The Raz/Shumaker Prairie
Schooner Book Prize in Fiction

EDITOR Kwame Dawes

VANISHED

STORIES   Karin Lin-Greenberg

UNIVERSITY OF NEBRASKA PRESS   LINCOLN

The University of Nebraska Press
is part of a land-grant institution
with campuses and programs
on the past, present, and future
homelands of the Pawnee, Ponca,
Otoe-Missouria, Omaha, Dakota,
Lakota, Kaw, Cheyenne, and
Arapaho Peoples, as well as those
of the relocated Ho-Chunk, Sac
and Fox, and Iowa Peoples.

Library of Congress
Cataloging-in-Publication Data
Names: Lin-Greenberg,
Karin, author.
Title: Vanished: stories /
Karin Lin-Greenberg.
Description: Lincoln: University
of Nebraska Press, [2022] | Series:
The Raz/Shumaker Prairie
Schooner Book Prize in Fiction
Identifiers: LCCN 2022009828
ISBN 9781496232571 (paperback)
ISBN 9781496233776 (epub)
ISBN 9781496233783 (pdf)
Subjects: BISAC: FICTION / Short
Stories (single author) | FICTION /
Women | LCGFT: Short stories.
Classification: LCC PS3612.
152 V36 2022 | DDC
813/.6—dc23/eng/20220412
LC record available at https://
lccn.loc.gov/2022009828

Set in Sabon Next by Laura Buis.
Designed by N. Putens.

CONTENTS

VANISHED

STILL LIFE

Today Alice's students will draw the pheasants. Alice unlocks the props closet in Bantam Hall on the downtown campus and sees the two taxidermied pheasants on a high shelf, exactly where she left them last semester. The pheasants were purchased by the Department of Art thirty-seven years ago, Alice's first year teaching at Juniper College. She places her tote bag on the floor and opens the brown stepladder in front of the metal shelf with the pheasants on top. She will ask the girls in her 10:00 a.m. Intermediate Drawing class to render the pheasants in pastel, but she knows the drawings will turn out poorly because these girls insist on buying the absolute cheapest supplies, garbage with too much filler and hardly any pigment. Bad supplies make bad art. Last week she overheard a student boasting about paying only two dollars for a box of pastels at Walmart. It is incomprehensible that these students think Walmart is an acceptable place to buy art supplies. One goes to Walmart to buy toothpaste and bug spray and cereal and kitty litter, not to buy the supplies with which you create art. But the girls in her classes don't actually aspire to be real artists; Alice knows they think her class is just a requirement to suffer through so they can get their degrees and get jobs.

"Oh, ma'am, ma'am, let me," calls a voice, and Alice turns and sees a boy with a wispy, struggling goatee rushing toward her.

"I'm perfectly capable," Alice says, and she puts one foot on the bottom step of the stepladder. Why is he calling her "ma'am"? Isn't it obvious she's a professor and owns a key to the closet? The boy looks at her as if she's an old vagrant who snuck into the building to pilfer supplies but, really, who would want to steal driftwood or cow skulls or cloth flowers? These items might be useful in a still life but not in real life.

"I'd better do it," says the boy as he walks toward her. "I'm Hutch. I'm the keeper of the props closet."

"The keeper of the props closet?" Alice cannot keep the incredulity out of her voice. Is he being paid to guard a locked closet containing objects of little to no monetary value? The closet is a large space—about half the size of a classroom—but it houses nothing any thief would want.

"It's my campus job," Hutch says, and Alice thinks this boy actually looks proud of himself. But it's not a necessary job, at least when professors in the department take the time to instruct their students about respecting the objects that inhabit the closet. But a quick glance at the mess here—the tablecloths bunched up in a corner, the upended armless mannequin, the brass tea kettle dented all over—tells Alice no one has talked to students about carefully putting things back in their proper spots after a still life has been disassembled.

"I didn't realize there was such a job," Alice says. She is uncomfortable now, with one foot still propped on the step, so she brings the other foot up.

"Oh, no, no, ma'am, I'll do it. I don't want you to hurt yourself." The boy has the nerve to reach out and touch her elbow, trying to guide her down the step as if she is a feeble blind person. Alice swats away his hand.

"Do you know how many years I've been fetching these birds from this shelf? And the other birds too?" Alice asks, sweeping her hand toward the Canada goose, and the pileated woodpecker

2

mounted to a tree stump, and the crow with the cracked beak, and the sleepy looking mallard.

"All the more reason to take a break and let me handle it," says Hutch. He scrambles up the ladder and Alice has a view of his hairy, knobby knees peeking out from baggy denim shorts. Her students have taught her that denim shorts are called jorts, a portmanteau of jeans and shorts, and they've said that only the nerdiest boys wear jorts. Her students are all at the Ilium campus, the old, battered campus where no one wants to teach anymore, especially not anyone in the Department of Art. The downtown campus is modern and bright, and the Department of Art there is housed in a newly constructed building featuring studio classrooms with excellent natural light pouring in from large windows, a darkroom for traditional photography, a lab with Macs with enormous screens for digital work, and even a 3-D printer. The real art degree, the serious sixty-credit major, is housed at the downtown campus.

"Wow," says Hutch, looking around at the top of the shelf, "it's dusty up here."

"Is dusting under the purview of the keeper of the props closet?"

"I could dust, I guess," Hutch says, and Alice wonders if he knows the meaning of the word "purview." Hutch descends the ladder and says, "I don't think I've seen you around before. Are you new?"

Alice laughs. She is most certainly not new. She's just never been assigned any classes at the downtown campus, so the students here think she's a stranger. She only shows up at the downtown campus for department meetings and to pick up objects from the props closet. The girls at the Ilium campus—the women's-only campus of Juniper, the original campus before the expansion downtown—are working toward art therapy degrees, not fine arts degrees. They are dabblers, who think art therapy is the easiest degree they can earn to get them a stable, good-paying job. Alice would love to teach the serious artists who are studying at the downtown campus, but what can Alice do when her younger colleagues are having gallery shows in New York City and she has done little—beyond throwing herself into her teaching—over her long career at Juniper? Is it her fault that the kind of figurative painting she does has gone out of vogue? And there was more than a decade in her thirties and forties when Alice cared for her ailing mother when she hadn't produced any paintings at all. After her mother passed, it hadn't seemed terribly important for Alice to continue her own artistic practice. She'd already earned tenure and could wallow at the rank of associate professor for the rest of her career.

"Can I bring the turkeys to your classroom for you?" asks Hutch, who is standing on the top step of the ladder, a pheasant under each arm. If he is not careful, he will crush their long tail feathers.

"They're pheasants."

"Right, okay," the boy says, but he seems unbothered by being corrected. This is likely because he is used to being either wrong or uninformed. "Can I bring the peasants to your classroom for you?" He descends the ladder and stands next to Alice.

She will not bother to educate Hutch on the difference between pheasants and peasants. "Are you an art student?" Alice asks.

The boy nods. "I'm a junior. Photography major."

Of course he is. Alice has always found the photography majors to be the most undisciplined; they are the ones who claim they don't need to learn to draw because it's not a required skill for photographers. What they don't understand is that learning to draw trains the hands and, more importantly, the eyes of any artist. Alice thinks photographers are only a small step above the art therapy majors. When the school first introduced art therapy as a major fifteen years ago, Alice told herself art therapy was a noble profession. She thought of her mother, of the dementia in her last years, and she wondered if perhaps an art therapist might have helped bring her some peace. When the art therapy degree was first approved by Juniper, Alice soothed herself about no longer teaching actual fine arts majors by telling herself the art therapy students were doing something good in the world. But lately the girls have seemed uninterested in helping, and mostly concerned with getting jobs after graduation.

"So where should I bring them?" asks Hutch, jutting his chin toward one of the pheasants he's holding.

"My classroom isn't on this campus," says Alice. "I teach on the Ilium campus."

"Really?" says Hutch, as if she's just said something stunning, as if she's told him Rembrandt is still alive. Scratch that—this boy likely hasn't heard of Rembrandt.

"Yes, really."

"Don't you have a props closet there?"

Alice doesn't say anything. Of course they don't have a props closet in Ilium. The one and only remaining art classroom on the Ilium campus is on the fourth floor of Wilty Hall, the building where the theater program is housed. There is an expansive props closet for the theater students, filled with costumes and objects that can be used in the dismal plays the students produce, but there is no props closet for the art therapy students, which is why Alice must raid the downtown props closet every time she wants to set up a still life. There is no elevator in Wilty Hall, so Alice must transport any props she needs to Ilium, haul them up four flights of stairs, and then lug them back downstairs and back to the downtown campus when she is done. Because Alice never learned to drive, she must take the ugly green campus-to-campus bus with the taxidermied animals as seatmates.

"Maybe I can talk to Professor Crews and see if he can give some of the department's budget for props to the Ilium campus," Hutch says, as if he's some benevolent benefactor, as if Alice has never asked for more funding for supplies, as if she's never asked if she can use some of the space currently allocated to the Theater Department for an art props closet at the Ilium campus. As if a boy in jorts who is struggling to grow facial hair can convince the department chair of what Alice has not been able to convince him to do. But she knows no funds will be allotted for supplies for her classes; she, like the Ilium campus and her art therapy students, is an afterthought in the department. She knows everyone is just waiting for her to retire. But then who will teach the girls in Ilium?

Alice hefts her tote bag up over one shoulder then says, "Please give me the pheasants," and Hutch hesitantly hands them over. She gets the pheasants settled under both of her arms by grabbing the wooden bases to which they are attached. She is careful not to crush any feathers. Both of these pheasants are males, with bright green heads, white collars around their necks, and coppery feathers on their bodies. They are beautiful birds.

"Do you just, like, put them in your trunk?" Hutch asks.

"I take the Green Bus."

"No!" Hutch says, his eyes wide. "Don't you drive?"

"I do not."

Hutch closes the stepladder and leans it back against the wall. "I thought everyone drove here."

"I have transported the pheasants on the bus plenty of times over the years to no ill effect."

"You need help getting them to the bus?" Hutch says. The expression on his face tells Alice he doesn't believe she can possibly make her way downstairs and to the corner where the bus will pick her up.

"I am just fine, thank you," Alice says. Then she realizes both of her hands are full and she will have to put the pheasants on the ground in order to lock the closet. The boy might as well put himself to some use. "Don't forget to lock the closet when you depart," she yells as she walks down the hall.

Alice always sits in the same seat on the bus, the one in the first row that's closest to the door. Years ago, when she first started teaching at Juniper, there was a handsome and pleasant bus driver named Paul, and he would converse with her during the twenty-minute drive. After a year Paul got a better-paying job driving buses for the city, and now the shuttle drivers are a rotating crew of young men who enjoy speeding through yellow lights and stomping on the brakes every time they have to stop.

Today Alice settles one pheasant on her lap and places the other on the seat next to her. She holds the base of the pheasant on the seat with her left hand so the bird will not topple down the aisle. Girls trudge onto the bus, and most of them look half asleep. Alice has heard the dorms in Ilium are not as nice as the downtown dorms, and this must be why most students insist on living downtown, even though doing so requires them to get up earlier than they deem humane in order to catch the shuttle for morning classes on the Ilium campus.

"Professor!" says Susanna Horton, as she climbs the steps of the bus. She stops in front of Alice's seat and points to the oversized men's undershirt she's wearing. In sloppy letters written in Sharpie are the words CAPILLARY PULL. Then there's a blob of marker beneath the words, the pigment pulling out in all directions, a demonstration of the concept of how ink naturally moves on a surface. "Capillary pull" is a term Alice taught her Intermediate Drawing class last week. She is befuddled as to why Susanna is wearing the term scribbled on an undershirt.

"It's the name of my band!" Susanna says. "We've been trying to figure out a band name for months, and when you said 'capillary pull' on Thursday I was like, 'Yes!' Jenna and Kimmy from class are also in the band."

"What instrument do you play?" Alice asks.

"Well," says Susanna, "the thing is we don't, really. We went to a bunch of thrift stores and got instruments, but we don't actually know how to play them."

"If you don't play instruments, how are you a band?"

"We're going for something atonal, so we don't actually want to learn how to play. We just make noise. I got a trombone. It's kind of rusted, but that doesn't really matter."

Alice has tried very, very hard to teach her students that skill is built through practice, that no one—well, maybe Picasso—springs from the womb as a highly skilled artist, and that hard work and constant practice lead to improvement. But it seems all her talking is for naught because these girls think they can actually be a band but not know how to play instruments. Maybe this is analogous to all the people who call themselves artists who don't make the effort to learn perspective or composition or color theory. If you say you're something nowadays, if you proclaim it loudly enough, well, perhaps you can convince the world that you are, in fact, the thing you say you are.

"I guess I should sit down," says Susanna, glancing back at the line of girls that has formed behind her. "But I just wanted to say thank you for naming our band."

Alice most certainly did not name Susanna's band, but she nods at Susanna and doesn't argue. Susanna shuffles to a seat near the rear of the bus, and Alice watches the rest of the students straggle onto the bus. As always, half of them are still wearing pajamas, as if these are acceptable clothes in which to attend class. Alice wonders what they think of her, riding the bus back and forth between downtown, where she lives, and the Ilium campus. She wonders if they feel sorry for her because she does not drive, but, really, it's possible to get by without driving if you live within walking distance of a supermarket and a drugstore and a library. Where else does Alice really need to go? When she was much younger, when her mother was still alive, there was an art supply store within walking distance of Alice's apartment, but it has been closed for decades now. It doesn't matter, though; she hasn't bought new supplies in a long time, and if she is somehow overcome with an urge to paint again, she can order anything she needs online. She never learned to drive because there simply was never a need. Even when her mother was sick, Alice didn't have to drive because there was a shuttle that came to get her mother, for free, to bring her to the hospital for her treatments, and Alice could ride along with her.

Alice is the only professor who takes the bus between campuses, and she wonders if the students find her sad and pathetic.

She is not married, never married, never had children. When she was a child she played the card game Old Maid with her mother, never thinking of what the name of the game meant. But now, she supposes, the students must think of her as an old maid, an old woman with no car and no family, who cares far too much about things they find unimportant, like paper texture and paint quality. They must think she cares so much about these things because there's nothing else in her life to care about.

Alice looks out the window as the bus passes through downtown. She likes to be driven, to not have to pay attention to directions. Being driven allows her to observe her surroundings in a way that would not be possible if she were driving. Alice believes artists should work on their observational skills, although her students nowadays spend most of their time with their noses in their phones and hardly any time looking at the world around them. Alice surveys the city through the bus's windows. In some parts the city is crumbling. The bus passes many homes with signs affixed to their exteriors that indicate the building is condemned, a red square with a white X through it. Many of these homes were once stately, once good, respectable places to live, but now they are unoccupiable, the glass panes of the windows gone, the stonework crumbling.

As they near the Ilium campus, Alice sees a group gathered outside Wilty Hall, and as the bus gets closer she sees the group consists of mostly students from her Intermediate Drawing class. She checks her watch and sees there are still ten minutes before class. The bus pulls into the parking lot across the street from Wilty Hall. Alice waits as the students file out of the bus, and then she hefts the pheasants up under her arms and disembarks. She walks toward the crowd and sees Tabatha Hanson, a junior colleague who teaches exclusively upper-level classes at the downtown campus. What is she doing in Ilium? In the art world Tabatha goes by Tabby Handz, which is a name Alice thinks is better suited for a cat than a human. Alice served on the committee that hired Tabby, and the rest of the committee overruled Alice's concerns about Tabby's obvious lack of skill; they all insisted Tabby would breathe new life into the program. Tabby is standing near the large brick wall of Wilty Hall that faces the street. Dozens of cans of spray paint are lined up by her high-top-clad feet.

"Hi there!" Tabby calls out as Alice storms toward her. Alice's progress is impeded by the two pheasants she is carrying, but she moves as quickly as she is able. Tabby is wearing a white jumpsuit with paint stains all over it, but Alice doesn't know if the stains are the result of creating art or if they're an affectation, like the rest of Tabby. Tabby's hair is completely shaved on one side of her head and the hair on the other side is long and dyed magenta. Alice's students look adoringly at Tabby, and Alice knows this is because they have seen the cover of *Artforum* with Tabby's face on it and know about the group show she was part of at the Brooklyn Museum of Art last year. These students don't particularly care about art, but they do care about success.

"What are you up to?" Alice asks.

"We're tagging this wall. Urban art, you know? Public art," Tabby says. Tabby's cover letter for her position at Juniper spoke of her great interest in graffiti and claimed graffiti is a way for artists outside of the mainstream art world to express themselves. She wrote, too, about the egalitarian nature of graffiti because one does not have to pay the price of admission to a museum to see it. She said if there had been more graffiti in the neighborhood where she grew up, she would have developed an earlier appreciation of art. Alice's colleagues ate up the things Tabby spewed in her letter and during her interview, but the problem is Tabby's pedigree—prep school in Massachusetts, expensive small liberal arts college in Maine, Ivy-league graduate school—is as mainstream as one can get. Of course Tabby never saw graffiti in the elite suburb where she grew up! During her campus interview, Tabby let it slip that her father was a judge for the state of Massachusetts and her mother owned a gallery in Boston. Tabby can dye her hair whatever colors she wants, but Alice can see the blonde roots and the blue eyes and the patrician features. During Tabby's interview, Alice wanted to tell everyone in the room about her own childhood—her father dying when she was just three from an accident at the textile factory where he worked, and then her mother struggling to keep them afloat as a waitress in two different restaurants—but she knew no one in her department wanted to hear about her past.

"Graffiti?" says Alice, looking down at the row of spray paint cans on the ground by Tabby's feet. "You know the school spent a great deal of money in the eighties and nineties scrubbing graffiti off this very wall." Ilium has gentrified in the last decade, and now there are four coffee shops and two wine bars and many restaurants that sell small plates of food for ridiculous sums of money. Many people who once lived in Ilium have been priced out. How will the current residents of Ilium—paying high rent for their apartments in brownstones—take to seeing a spray painted wall?

Tabby laughs, as if Alice has told a joke. "Your students have agreed to help."

"My students have pheasants to draw." Alice hefts up the pheasants, who've grown increasingly heavy. She is offended Tabby spoke to her students and asked them to do a project without her permission. And what is Tabby doing in Ilium? Doesn't she have classes to teach at the downtown campus?

"Oh, please, can we help Tabby?" says Susanna. "This is *so* cool! I can't believe we have the opportunity to be part of a Tabby Handz art production. We're going to be all over the Internet."

"Oh, rad shirt," says Tabby, pointing at Susanna's defaced undershirt.

"It's the name of my band. We're playing at the Bowl Hole on Friday at ten. You should come."

"That sounds amazing," says Tabby, and Alice notes that Tabby has not actually committed to attending. Alice feels insulted she was not invited even though, had she been, she would not have gone to whatever unsavory place Bowl Hole is.

"I had a lesson planned about color today. High key, low key, hue, intensity, temperature," Alice says.

Tabby stares at Alice for a few seconds as if she is unfamiliar with those terms. More of Alice's Intermediate Drawing students have gathered outside the building. "You could still teach them the terms using spray paint. I've got a whole array of colors here."

"Do you have a plan for what's going to be painted?" Alice asks. "Do you have sketches?"

"Planning takes away spontaneity. It saps energy from art."

"You never plan what you'll paint?" When she still painted, Alice always planned: first small thumbnails in a sketchbook, then larger sketches on big sheets of paper, then an underpainting on canvas, and then finally the oil painting, which usually took several months to complete.

"Never," says Tabby with a solemnity Alice finds ridiculous.

Alice sighs and puts the pheasants down onto the sidewalk. Her arms are sore and she cannot hold the birds any longer. Her students have all flung their portfolios containing their drawing pads and sketches from this semester onto the sidewalk. Alice suddenly feels weary, unsure if she can make it up the four flights of stairs to her overheated classroom, so she nods. "Fine, fine. They can paint the wall."

"Yay, this is going to be super fun!" says Susanna, and she claps and the other girls gathered around Tabby also clap, as if something wonderful and miraculous has happened.

"Just please be careful of the pheasants. I need to return them in the same condition I got them in, so please no one spray paint them." Alice moves the pheasants to under a stop sign at the corner of the block, as far away from the wall as she can put them while still being able to keep an eye on them. She rejoins the crowd surrounding Tabby.

"I bet you'd be allowed to keep them in your office here," says Tabby, pointing to the pheasants. Tabby's fingernails are painted with a garish blue polish. "I think you're the only one who ever uses them. Or any of the birds."

"The pheasants need to be available to everyone in the department. How else will our students learn about avian anatomy?"

"I'm not sure how important it is for them to learn avian anatomy," says Tabby. "Here," she says, swooping down and picking up a can of spray paint. She shoves the can toward Alice.

"What am I supposed to do with that?"

"Use it."

"Oh," says Alice, as she wraps a hand around the can. It feels cold under her palm.

"Grab some paint!" shouts Tabby to Alice's students. "Large movements, don't think too much, be bold, be vibrant! And switch colors often with your friends! We're all friends here, right?"

The girls shout "Right!" as if Tabby is an evangelical leader they have been brainwashed to follow.

"Let's go!" shouts Tabby, and she runs to the wall and releases a stream of purple paint. Alice wants to know whether Tabby can actually draw. If she were to lock Tabby in a room and tell her she could only leave if she could draw a realistic-looking pheasant, could she do it? Could she get the proportions correct? Everyone is enamored of Tabby's squiggles and blobs, but are these just a way of covering lack of skill? In an interview in the *New York Times*, Tabby cited Banksy as an influence, but there's a big difference between Tabby and Banksy. Banksy is anonymous, but Tabby thrives on being known and being seen. Her last gallery show was called *Street Stories* and featured photographs of the walls Tabby tagged. In the photographs, she is posing in front of each wall in her paint-splattered jumpsuit, her arms crossed, glaring at the camera. Why does she need to be in every photo? Why can't the work just exist without her glowering face in every single picture? Alice is certain

Tabby is in constant contact with Juniper's office of marketing so they can feature her in all their publications. Tabby is an excellent publicist for her own work. And maybe that's all being an artist is about nowadays; maybe it's more about promoting yourself than producing quality work.

Alice can smell the spray paint in the air and she coughs from the fumes. She stands still and watches the brick wall fill with color. Of course no one is thinking of the relationships between colors. If they'd planned just a little, there could be pleasing color relationships, some color vibration. Instead, the wall is a mess; a disgusting, undisciplined mess. Her students are laughing, jumping, spraying. Why do the students seem so excited, so filled with energy in a way they never are in her classes? She sets the can of spray paint Tabby gave her down on the sidewalk.

Tabby walks over to Alice. She shakes a can of paint, and Alice can hear the marble inside clink up and down. "I have the chair's permission. Crews told me it was fine, that he doesn't care about this building. He said it would be good to give it some color. So don't worry, we're not going to get arrested or anything."

"I wasn't worried about getting arrested," Alice says. And, anyway, if they did happen to find themselves arrested, Alice is certain Tabby's father, the judge, would get them out of trouble.

"The school photographer is scheduled to come in half an hour. We'll probably get on the homepage of Juniper's website."

"For defacing a wall?" Alice says, and Tabby says nothing in response. Tabby keeps shaking her paint can, and Alice wonders whether Tabby is about to spray her with the paint. Then she sees something behind Tabby. "No!" she shouts. There is a dog, large and gray, with long legs, who is nosing around the pheasants. Alice hurries to the birds.

"I'm sorry," says the owner, a short woman who looks to be around Alice's age. Her hair is dyed an unnatural and flat black. She tugs hard on the dog's orange leash. "Sylvester is just curious. I think he's got some hunting dog in him and he can't help himself when he sees birds."

Alice looks at the dog's white muzzle. It's funny, she thinks, how dogs gray just like humans do. Sylvester is sniffing the tail of one of the pheasants. The dog seems slow and lumbering, not what Alice pictures when she thinks of a hunting dog. She watches the dog continue to sniff the pheasants and wonders if they ever encountered a dog in the wild. Had they ever lived free in the outdoors? Or had they been confined somewhere, the plan since their birth for them to be stuffed and mounted on wooden boards? "My students were supposed to draw the pheasants today, but instead they're doing this," Alice says, waving toward the vandalized brick wall. It feels like a waste, suddenly, for these pheasants to have given their lives and for no one—besides Alice—to find any use for them.

"Your students look like they're having fun," says the woman. "No, no, Sylvester," she says, pulling the dog's leash as he lifts a paw.

"I suppose they are having fun," says Alice. But fun is not what life is about. Life is about discipline and dedication and striving to improve. It isn't about being the loudest and boldest and the one having the most fun.

The dog is still nosing around the pheasants and Alice sees a wet pink tongue emerge, and before he can lick the birds, Alice bends down and picks up the pheasants. "I'll just get them out of the way," she says, "before harm can befall them."

The woman nods and the dog pulls her toward the mess of girls who are madly covering the wall in spray paint, and she says, "Well, it'll be nice to see some color up on the wall when I walk Sylvester in the mornings."

Alice stands near the stop sign with the pheasants under her arms and watches as the woman and dog move down the street. The dog's legs are bowed, and Alice can tell from his stiff gait that he has arthritis. She looks down at the birds and thinks of how they are frozen in time, how they look nearly the same as they did decades ago, only a little worse for the wear. Alice watches Susanna, who has spray paint all over her CAPILLARY PULL shirt, who is laughing and spray-painting, and she sees that some trails of paint have dribbled onto the sidewalk. Does the school own the sidewalk or does the city of Ilium?

The Green Bus rolls down the street for the 10:30 drop-off and pick-up. Alice's girls, all of them, don't seem to remember they showed up today for her class. After the lesson on color, she planned to show them how to draw feathers that look so realistic a viewer would have to resist the urge to stick out a finger to touch the drawing. But it is clear no one is interested in learning what Alice has to teach.

The bus stops, the doors open with a pneumatic hiss, and a handful of students spill out. When the bus is empty, Alice climbs back on with the pheasants and sits in her usual seat. Alice looks out the window at her students and Tabby, at the paint-drenched wall, at all of them having so much goddamn fun. She wonders if Hutch and his jorts will be waiting by the props closet when she returns the pheasants; she wonders if he'll ask her why she's back so early, as if he's someone to whom she needs to explain her choices. Well, here is a choice: she will bring the pheasants back to her apartment downtown and will climb a step stool—without assistance—and will place them on top of the tall bookshelf in her living room. She will not say anything about where they are to her colleagues, and she will wait and see if anyone inquires about them. But of course they will not. No one else uses the pheasants, no one else has touched them in years. No one will even notice they are missing.

HOUSEKEEPING

Franco Tyrone's suicide at The Corvid Motel was the biggest thing that had ever happened in Galaville. Franco had been in town to film an episode of his television show, *Finding the Heart of America*. The day after he killed himself, he was supposed to talk to the LaBella brothers, who baked made-from-scratch fruit pies in an old pizza oven, and then he was supposed to interview Dizzy Garrity about tapping maple trees for syrup, and then he was scheduled to meet with me at Galaville Orchards and film me talking about how I make our famous cider doughnuts. I should say the dough-nuts were not actually famous, but a sign in our front window declared FAMOUS CIDER DO-NUTS, so Franco was supposed to call them famous and maybe, once they were mentioned on TV, they would become famous and people from the city driving upstate to admire the fall foliage would stop and buy dozens. Like the doughnuts, I was supposed to be on television and, like the doughnuts, I thought I would get a little famous. Franco always made it seem as if the people he talked to on *Finding the Heart of America* mattered, and the places they came from mattered too. I'd hoped being on television might make me someone interesting, might make it seem like I wasn't only thought of as just the smart, uptight girl, the nerd destined to be valedictorian of Galaville High.

But, of course, there was no interview with Franco. My sister worked as a maid at The Corvid, and when she went to clean Franco's room at noon, she knocked and then shouted "Housekeeping!" three times and when there was no answer, she entered the room and discovered him hanging. She was interviewed by the Albany news stations and then, because Franco was famous, she was interviewed by the national news shows. Everyone wanted to talk to the girl who'd discovered Franco's body. "It was terrible," she repeated in every interview. "It was the worst thing I ever saw. And I'm just so sorry for his family and friends." When the reporter from Albany with the crooked tie and slicked down hair asked Tess if she had any suspicions about why Franco had killed himself, she tilted her head and said, "How can anyone know that?"

Because Tess was beautiful, she became a meme, screenshots from the news interviews of her outside the motel appearing all over the Internet. In these screenshots, Tess was standing below the wooden THE CORVID MOTEL sign with the silhouette of a crow, her hair blowing in the breeze. Her image was superimposed with phrases like "When Life Gives You Lemons, Make Sure Your Hair Is On Point" or "Stay Sexy Through Tragedy!" She became known as the "Hot Crier" online. A few weeks after Franco's suicide, the Internet spent more time talking about my sister's cheekbones and lush cascade of dark curls blowing in the wind than they did about what had driven Franco to end his life. His story was sad and tragic, of course, but not fully unexpected. He'd had a few good years, a few famous years, but fame and money don't solve anyone's problems. He had a history with severe depression, starting in the days when he was a PhD student. When he turned fifty, he took an extended leave from his university teaching job, and to keep busy he traveled the country by car and started a blog about under-the-radar places and people in America. Then the blog blew up and then the Travel Network came calling and he became a star and officially quit his job teaching American history to college students. But I guess what haunts you always haunts you, and some people are just too haunted to push aside what gnaws at their minds. So there wasn't much more to say about Franco after the initial shock and sadness, but Tess, well, she seemed like someone fascinating whose story would continue on, a young woman with model good looks wasting her life away in upstate New York working as a motel maid and caring for her sixteen-year-old sister.

Tess was my legal guardian. My parents were alive but out of the picture, as they were unsuited for the responsibility of parenthood and could not resist the lure of opioids. That's all I'll say about them. Their story is generic enough to be a cliché, and I prefer not to dwell on the details. When she turned eighteen—six years ago—Tess became my legal guardian, and since graduating from high school she'd been working at The Corvid Motel, which provided enough of an income for us to live very modestly. I contributed to our family of two by working at Galaville Orchards after school and on weekends and in the summers. I worked in The Orchard Store in the fall and winter, hawking apple-flavored comestibles and country-kitsch items (potholders, candles, aprons, Christmas tree ornaments) meant to evoke a Norman Rockwell America that never actually existed. In the spring and summer I worked in the orchards, picking fruit and directing the customers who came for pick-your-own to suitable aisles of trees or bushes. It was, of course, not a privileged upbringing, but it worked for us until our lives got turned upside down.

I suppose I shouldn't have been terribly surprised when the producers of *Great Catch!* came calling a few weeks after Franco's suicide, asking Tess if she wanted to be a contestant. By then everyone in America with an Internet connection and any interest in popular culture knew who she was. The producers told her she'd be a fan favorite with her sad backstory, and if she went far enough on the show without actually winning there was a good chance she could be the lead on the next season of *Great Lady Catch!*, where twenty men competed to become "the one."

You know *Great Catch!* and *Great Lady Catch!*, I'm sure. On *Great Catch!* twenty women vie for the heart of one man, and each week several are eliminated in what the show calls "the quest for love." The show culminates in a proposal. Never mind that out of the twenty-seven final couples the show has produced over the years, only four have made it to the altar.

Shortly before Tess found Franco's body she'd broken up with Ricky, her boyfriend of four years, so she was single and free to be a contestant. (Although, according to the gossip sites, plenty of contestants have come on the show while dating someone else; the lure of television and the possible fame it might bring is too much for some people to turn down.) I always pretended to be annoyed by Ricky, but he wasn't a bad guy. He was an auto mechanic and he kept our car running. He could fix the things that broke around our house, clean the gutters, capture and take outdoors the spiders that neither Tess nor I wanted to touch. He liked watching videos of idiot animals online. When he was at our house he'd always call out to me, even if I was in a different room, and say stuff like, "Look at this raccoon falling off a roof!" then hold up his phone to me, and we'd cackle about the dumb raccoon together. Tess didn't find animal videos amusing. "What percent of the Internet do you think is taken up by animal videos?" she asked one day, and Ricky said, "Not enough of it."

"You're leaving me to go to California to film a show?" I asked after Tess got off the phone with the producers of *Great Catch!*. I'd listened to the entire conversation—her side of it—and was able to piece together what was being asked of her.

"Elaine will look in on you," she said. "It'll only be for three weeks."

Elaine was our neighbor. She was sixty-two years old, was an accountant for the State of New York, owned three malodorous ferrets, and had a fondness for polyester clothing for both work and play.

"The issue here isn't my care and maintenance. I'm self-sufficient," I said. "I'm like a cactus. Here, but not needy."

"This is an opportunity, Benny," Tess said. "This fell into my lap, and if I say no, then what? I don't want to work at The Corvid forever. It's maybe a way out. For both of us." In fact, Tess hadn't been back to The Corvid since she found Franco. The manager of the motel had generously given her a week off with pay, but then Tess couldn't make herself return after that week was over. She said she just couldn't slide a key card into a lock, couldn't push down the door handle and open a door, not knowing what was waiting for her inside. By the time the producers of *Great Catch!* called, Tess hadn't worked in almost a month.

"I don't want Elaine looking in on me. Can you ask Ricky to do it?"

"I haven't really talked to him since we broke up. And I think it'd be weird if he took care of you. People might think it was improper. A teenage girl and a twenty-five-year-old guy shouldn't be hanging out alone. People talk in this town."

I sighed, loudly and dramatically, in case it wasn't clear yet to Tess that I was appalled about what she was going to do. "Funny that you care about impropriety while being willing to go on television to stick your tongue down some dude's throat," I said.

"Stop, Benny," she said.

"Stop what?" I said, as innocently as I could.

"Just stop your Bennyness. The judgmental stuff. Just please stop."

Of course Tess went to L.A. to film *Great Catch!*. I told her that Hudson Plum—the supposedly great catch starring on this season of the show—was a goober, but she didn't care. I knew there were more damning pejoratives than goober, but Hudson was so banal that he did not warrant a more severe descriptor. Hudson had been rejected by Samantha "Sammi" Jensen, the star of last season's *Great Lady Catch!* after he brought her home to visit his family, and the audience felt sympathy for Hudson's heartbreak even though the family visit made it clear he was a spoiled trust fund kid. After college, he'd embarked on a career as a rapper named H-Plummy. A *white* rapper. A white rapper who grew up in a mansion in Connecticut. There were some kids like him at my high school, white boys who didn't believe they had any culture of their own so they liked to appropriate the cultures of other people whose backgrounds were filled with much more struggle and strife than theirs. Hudson's sob story—because everyone has to have one on these shows—was that no one took him seriously as a rapper because he was rich and hadn't had much hardship in his life. Based on the snippets of his rapping shown on *Great Lady Catch!*, I knew the issue was really one of utter lack of talent, not the fact that he was rich and white and privileged. Let's just say he was no Eminem. He wasn't even Macklemore.

So Tess went away to try to win H-Plummy's heart and I kept going to school and working at Galaville Orchards. Elaine stopped by every evening to make sure I was still, in fact, alive. Sometimes she brought food, dense, cheesy casseroles, but I threw them away because I found a ferret hair in the first casserole she brought over. It was quiet at home without Tess, who was always there after I returned from school or work. I wondered for the first time whether Tess had taken the job at The Corvid because it was compatible with my school schedule. Now, of course, I didn't need anyone home with me after school, but when I was younger, even though I was capable of making my own after-school snack, I liked having Tess home, cutting up an apple for me, slathering each slice with peanut butter, handing me the apple slices on a plate, and asking how my day went.

I got to talk to Tess on the phone every few days. The contestants weren't allowed to have their own cell phones, but the few young mothers (who would inevitably be kept around for a few weeks so H-Plummy wouldn't seem completely coldhearted for cutting them immediately, but what twenty-eight-year-old man wants a ready-made family and the baggage of another man's child?) were allowed to call home and speak to their children, and because Tess was my legal guardian, we got to talk too. But she couldn't say very much because there would always be a handler in the room with her, so mostly she asked questions about my day and was elusive with answering my questions about what she was up to.

"Is he as much of a goober as I think he is?" I asked the first time we got to talk.

"We haven't talked much one-on-one," she said. "But he seems nice."

"The crossing guard is nice. One of Elaine's ferrets is nice. Nice isn't worth much."

"All right, Benny," Tess said. "I'm calling just to check and make sure you're okay."

"I'm okay," I said. "I'm fine. It's pretty great having the run of the house. How many girls do you have to share a bathroom with?"

"All right," she said again. "That's all I needed to know. I just need to know that you're okay. And you have the number to call in case you need me, right?"

"I'm fine," I said. "You just go and fall in love with H-Plummy, and then we'll have his rich family buy us things. That's the plan, right?"

"I'm glad you're doing okay," said Tess. "I'll call again when I can." And then she was gone, even though I hadn't said good-bye yet.

I waited by the home phone each night to see if Tess would call, and I kept checking my cell to see if I'd missed a message, but she didn't call for three nights, and I wondered if she was having a great time and had forgotten about me. Even though Hudson was a loser of epic proportions, the other girls were probably fun, and Tess could be having the best time of her life without me. Tess didn't have many friends in Galaville. She was smart in high school, and she hung out with the other smart girls. And those girls were long gone. Everyone knew Galaville was a dead-end town, and if you had more than two brain cells, you got out. If you didn't want to move too far away there were some colleges near Albany, and if you wanted to get out and never look back you kept driving until New York State was far behind you in the rearview mirror. The people besides Ricky that Tess spent the most time with in the last few years were the other maids from The Corvid, but most of them were older, complained incessantly about sore backs and cracked skin on their hands, or were from other countries and barely spoke English. Sometimes there were younger girls who worked at the motel for a few months, but it was hard and messy work, and if other opportunities came up, they would jump at them. I thought about Tess living in a mansion in L.A. with all the other contestants, and I thought how this might be her idea of heaven. She could talk to these other girls about things I didn't care about—makeup and hair products and women's magazines—and it would be like a three-week slumber party. It didn't even matter if she liked Hudson or not—it was just an escape from life at The Corvid and life at home with me.

When Tess finally called again, her voice sounded pinched, embarrassed. "I need a favor," she said.

"Do you need me to send you something?" I asked. She'd packed nearly the entire contents of her closet before she left for California. She'd also packed eight cocktail dresses for the champagne ceremonies, during which each contestant who was being asked to stay was offered a glass of champagne. (There were theories online about how the contestants the star liked the most were offered the bubbliest flutes of champagne, but I was unsure if there was validity to those theories.) We, of course, did not have money for cocktail dresses, but Ricky's older sister had competed in the pageant circuit for a few years when she was in high school, and there were dresses left in a closet at their parents' home and she said Tess could have them. I knew Tess had contacted Ricky's sister directly so she wouldn't have to go through Ricky because she didn't want to tell him she was going to be a contestant on *Great Catch!*. The dresses were all a little short for Tess since she was taller than Ricky's sister, but they'd have to do. They were also about fifteen years out of date, but maybe they were so out of date they were coming back into fashion.

"I need you to write me something," Tess said. "A poem."

I know I said Tess was smart, but she was more a science and math person, and I was more of a reading and writing person. Put our brains together and we'd be a genius. I was smart enough to get As in math and science classes, but I was never going to break a mathematical code. Tess was able to write five-paragraph essays and identify literary terms, but ask her to do something creative like write a poem and she'd have some trouble.

"Why do you need a poem?" I said.

"Well, sort of a poem. It's more like a rap."

"You need *me* to write you a rap?"

"Hudson and I have been getting along. We had a one-on-one date. He wrote me a rap and the producers were thinking I could write one for him for our next one-on-one. They wrote one for me, but I thought you could do a lot better."

"Can I hear it?" I said. "The one they wrote for you?"

"Oh, I don't know," she said.

"If you rap it for me, I'll write you a rap."

"I'll *read* it to you. I'm not rapping it for you."

"But they're going to make you rap, aren't they? There's no way they'll let you just read a poem as if you're reciting Emily Dickinson."

"I'll read it to you. Take it or leave it."

"Take it."

I heard Tess sigh, then I heard the sound of unfolding paper. "Okay," she said. "Here it is:

> Yo, Hudson Plum,
> I ain't dumb.
> Heard you like like me,
> And I like like you too.

Got all the feels over you.
My champagne flute flows over
I'm luckier than a four-leaf clover
I'm luck luck luck-eeeee
'cause I love this love between you and me.
Yo, Hudson, when you gonna
get down on one knee?"

"I might vomit," I said. "Suddenly I'm feeling extremely queasy."

"I *know*," she said. "And I know you can do better."

"That's not really a compliment."

"Look," Tess said, her voice low. "This will help me advance. It'll give me a storyline, make me a frontrunner. Could you write me something that's not totally embarrassing?"

"I can write you a sonnet," I said. "Let me know if you'd prefer Shakespearian or Petrarchan. How you choose to deliver it is up to you, but I would highly suggest not rapping. All anyone is saying about you online right now is that you're beautiful. You don't want to become a joke once the episode airs."

"I know," said Tess. "Of course I know that." She sighed, then said, "I miss you, Benny."

I waited a few seconds without answering, and then Tess said, "Benny? You there? Hello?"

"I'm here," I said. "Of course I'm here. Where else would I go?"

The next day Ricky came into The Orchard Store during his lunch hour. He had grease all over his gray jumpsuit and black streaks on his face. He took off his baseball cap as if he were entering a church. I hadn't seen him in over two months, since he and Tess had broken up. He looked tired and older and the skin on his forehead where the baseball cap had covered it was a few shades lighter than the rest of his face.

"I'm here for doughnuts," he said, before I even said hello. "A dozen."

"We only have three left," I said. "There was a big group on a school field trip that passed through earlier. They bought the rest."

"I'll take the three then," said Ricky. "I was going to get a dozen for the guys at the shop."

"Did you screw up? If you screwed up you can't cut up the doughnuts into quarters and make people share them."

"Why would you say that, Benny?" He rubbed his hand across his forehead and left another dark streak. "Why would you automatically assume I screwed up?"

"It's just that people don't usually go around buying doughnuts to give away unless they screwed up. If you can wait a while, I can make more. It'll take a few minutes for the oil to get hot enough."

"I've gotta get back. I'll just take the three."

"Will you get in trouble if you're a little late? Would you get fired?"

"I'm kind of in charge nowadays."

"You are?"

"Tess didn't tell you?"

I shook my head.

"Mike had a stroke, so I've been in charge for a few months."

"Is Mike going to be okay?" Mike owned Rooney's Tires and Repairs. He had worked there most of his life after inheriting the shop from his father. He wasn't that old, maybe fifty, not old enough to stop working.

"He's doing rehab now. Physical therapy. But I don't know. I'm trying not to think too far into the future."

"Do you make the guys call you 'Boss Man'?"

"I make them call me 'Sir.' And they have to bow when I walk into the room."

He smiled, seemed to relax a little, and felt more like the Ricky I used to know. "Hey, so have you heard from Tess? I heard from my sister she's out in California." He said it casually, as if he didn't really care whether I'd heard from her or not, but then I realized the whole reason he came into the shop was so he could ask about Tess. The doughnuts were just an excuse.

"Yeah, she calls every few days."

"So is she head over heels in love with H-Plummy yet?" He said it like a joke, but I could tell that all of it bothered him.

"He wrote her a rap. That's all I know," I said. Ricky looked sad, so I added, "I don't think she really likes him."

"Right," he said. He put his hat back on his head, then adjusted it so the brim was straight. "So the doughnuts? I'll take those three."

I packed them up for him in a white paper bag and handed him his change.

"See you around, Benny," he said and he left. I wondered when I'd see him next. He'd been such a part of our lives for four years, and now we never saw each other. The only time I'd ever see him now was if we accidentally ran into each other.

All afternoon I made more doughnuts, even though Mrs. Crenshaw, who ran the Orchard Store, told me to slow down, said we weren't going to sell them all before closing. If there were doughnuts left at the end of the day I was allowed to take them home, but usually there were only one or two left over and I'd eat them on my walk back to the house. But I wanted there to be a lot of extras that day because I wanted to go to the repair shop with a dozen doughnuts. They'd give me an excuse to hang out with Ricky.

After work I walked to Rooney's Tires and Repairs with a large paper sack filled with fresh doughnuts. The warm grease from the doughnuts seeped through the paper, and I wished I'd brought a stack of napkins with me too. My phone rang as I was walking, and I had to stop, sit on a big rock by the side of the road, and set the greasy bag on the ground.

"Do you have the rap written? Or the poem, or whatever you want to call it?" said Tess.

"You only asked me to write it three days ago. I have homework to do. And I'm working every afternoon this week," I said. "I'm not some poem-on-demand service."

Tess sighed. "Since we talked there's been another champagne ceremony. The producers said I have to present him with a rap before the next one. And that's in two days. If I don't share a rap with him, I might not make it to the overnight dates."

"Are you going to sleep with him during the overnight date?" I asked.

"That's none of your business, Benny," she said.

"Even if you don't, the show will insinuate that you did." They always showed the contestants the next morning in bed, the sheets rumpled, their hair askew.

"I know what I signed up for," Tess said.

"It's just that if you have sex with him and you're only really interested in all of this for money and opportunities, you're kind of prostituting yourself."

Tess was silent for a few moments, then said, "I told you, I know what I'm getting into. And I know that all of this can make things better for us."

"If I write you a poem does that make me an accessory to prostitution?"

"Don't be this way, Benny."

"Guess who came to the orchard shop today?"

"I don't know. Who? Someone famous?"

"The only famous person who ever came to Galaville offed himself."

"I know you're mad that I'm away, but don't act like this. I'll stop calling if you do. I'll just call Elaine and ask her if you're doing okay."

And that was the threat that made me change my tune. I didn't want Tess to stop calling. "I'm doing okay," I said. "I'm cooking real things for dinner, not just microwaving stuff. I made chicken piccata last night. I found the recipe online."

"That's good," said Tess. "That's really good. So who was it?"

"Who was what?"

"Who came into the store?" she said.

"Oh, just Mr. Gallagher. He bought some apple butter." I didn't want to talk about Ricky right then, so I made up the lie about Mr. Gallagher coming to the store. I thought it might upset Tess to know Ricky was asking about her, and it might upset her more to know I was on my way to see him with a sack of doughnuts. Mr. Gallagher taught ninth- and tenth-grade English, and both Tess and I had been in his class. We'd both loved him for his enthusiastic readings of poetry even though the other kids made fun of him behind his back. "Do I dare to eat a peach?" other kids belted in the cafeteria, holding up fruit they'd pulled out of their brown paper lunch bags, then snorting with laughter at their imitations of Mr. Gallagher. But Tess and I thought it was nice that Mr. Gallagher cared so much about poetry that when he read it, his eyes closed and he had all the words memorized, like a favorite song.

"He was a good teacher," said Tess. "You know he emailed me a couple of times in the past few years, encouraging me to apply to college?"

I hadn't known that. "Did you?" I asked.

Tess laughed. "Of course not," she said. "How?"

There was so much packed into that one-word question, so much about how it would ever be possible for Tess to afford college, go to college, and so much unsaid about how my presence, my always-present presence, stood in the way of Tess moving forward.

"I'll get you that poem by tomorrow, okay?" I said. I wanted to give Tess something, even though I knew even a mediocre poem would signal to Hudson that Tess had fallen for him so much that she was moved to write verse. But I wanted to write her a poem that would stun both Mr. Gallagher and H-Plummy with its depth and insight into the human condition. I wanted Tess to win the show and be happy and never have to work again, and I wanted her to lose and come home. I wanted a lot of things, most of them in opposition to each other.

When I got to Rooney's there were no customers in the waiting area and only Bo was at one of the computers, logging something from a stack of receipts.

"Benny! Long time no see," he said. He had cinnamon sugar in his goatee and the empty bag of doughnuts was next to him. Some afternoons Tess and I would visit Ricky in the shop, so everyone there knew us. I hadn't been to the shop since Ricky and Tess broke up, so that's why I didn't know about Mike's stroke.

"Is Ricky here?" I asked.

"Back office," said Bo, pointing backward with his thumb. "Go ahead."

I made my way through the door with the EMPLOYEES ONLY sign on it and walked down the hallway leading to the office. Ricky was watching something on the computer, completely absorbed. Behind him there was a calendar with a photograph of a piglet on it, something new since the last time I'd been back there. When I got closer I saw that it was from the Humane Society, the kind you get for donating money, and I wondered if Ricky had given money to them. I got all the way to the doorway without Ricky noticing me, and then when he did he quickly stopped whatever video was playing, which plunged the room into silence.

"Hey, hey, Benny!" he said, sounding nervous and guilty. I wondered if he'd been watching porn. Was that what the men who worked at Rooney's did when it wasn't busy?

"Are you watching porn?" I asked, as I made my way around to the back of the desk. "Did Tess break up with you because you're addicted to porn?"

Ricky looked at me as if I were insane, and clicked on his browser so it filled the entire screen. He was watching a clip from *Finding the Heart of America* on YouTube. His eyes looked teary and I felt bad about my accusation. "I brought you doughnuts. A dozen, like you wanted before." I held them up in front of his face.

"Everyone's gone home already," he said. "Except for Bo, and he ate the three I bought earlier."

"You can leave them out for the morning, even though they'll be a little stale." I didn't care if they got stale, though; the doughnuts were just my way of saying "I miss you, I wish you still came around the house, I want to watch videos of raccoons with you, I know it's weird if we hang out now, but I wish we could."

I put the bag on top of a metal filing cabinet. I knew there would be a grease spot left on the cabinet, but there was nothing I could do about it.

"You ever watch this show?" Ricky said, clicking play on the video and then muting the volume. I pulled up a folding chair next to him and we watched Franco Tyrone in the home kitchen of an old woman in West Virginia. Franco and the woman poked wooden spoons into a big pot of some sort of brown meat boiling on the stove.

"Yeah," I said. I'd been a fan of Franco's since the show started, and when I learned Franco was coming to Galaville I rewatched a lot of episodes, studied them, watched the way he was with people, the way he could make even the humblest place or person seem like something special and worth filming.

We were quiet for a little while and watched the silent action on the screen, an episode I hadn't seen before, where Franco and the old woman chopped an onion and then a carrot and tilted the chopping board so the onion and carrot went into the pot with the boiling meat. And then I saw the title of the episode, and said, "Oh," and pointed to the screen. "A Raccoon in Every Pot."

"I know," said Ricky, and then he started to weep, and I looked around for tissues and couldn't find any, so I just sat there and did nothing and kept my eyes on the screen, where Franco was now dancing in the kitchen with the old woman, lifting one arm and spinning her, and she was delighted and had her eyes closed, and I thought about Mr. Gallagher reading us "The Love Song of J. Alfred Prufrock" and how there were so few moments in life when you're so happy, so satisfied that you want to close your eyes and smile. Ricky tried to make a joke of it, said, "Not the kind of raccoon video we usually watch, huh?," and I shook my head.

"Are you sad they're eating a raccoon? Is that what's going on?" I said, even though I knew his sadness was about something bigger.

"Did Tess tell you I was addicted to porn?" he said. "Is that why she said we broke up? Because that's not true at all."

I shook my head. "You just looked so guilty when I stepped into the office. Like I caught you doing something you shouldn't be doing."

"I should have been working on the books but I can't stop watching *Finding the Heart of America*. I don't know why. Like it's going to give me any answers about anything."

"About Franco?"

First Ricky shook his head, then he nodded, said, "Maybe. I mean, how can you care so much about people, act like everyone is important, act like everyone's story is a good one, and then do what he did? Doesn't this mean he thought his own story was worthless? Do you know he has a daughter? She's twelve."

"I didn't know that," I said. It was awful, this left-behind daughter. Ricky kept crying, and I got up and went to the bathroom down the hall, came back with a stack of rough brown paper towels, handed a few to Ricky, and put the rest under the bag of doughnuts. He wiped his eyes and face with the paper towels, crumpled them, and dropped them into a wastebasket. He sniffled hard, as if he was trying to suck all his sadness back into his skull.

"Why'd you break up?" I asked.

"Tess never told you?"

"I guess there are a lot of things she doesn't tell me."

"I asked her to marry me."

I was stunned. If I were a cartoon character, my eyeballs would have popped out of my head. Why had Tess kept this information from me? Why would she consider a proposal grounds for a breakup? If Mr. Gallagher were here he'd say the fact that Tess was filming *Great Catch!* with the hope of being proposed to shortly after turning down Ricky's proposal would be an example of irony. "She broke up with you because you proposed?"

Ricky shrugged. "She said she wanted something more than Galaville and wanted to know if I'd ever leave. I told her I have a good job here, my family's here. My life is here, you know? And, look," he said, pointing to the screen, "just because someone leaves home, travels, sees the world, it doesn't mean they end up happy."

I nodded. I always thought I would be the one who'd get out, had always imagined Tess would be here, ready to welcome me home anytime I wished. I had pictured myself older, coming home to visit, and Tess cutting up an apple for me, spreading peanut butter on every slice, asking me to tell her about my exciting life. Tess was an inextricable part of my conception of Galaville, and maybe it was that way for Ricky too. Sure, she'd come back for a while, try to make things work, but Galaville would feel different, small and stifling. I knew how these things went, how the people cast on reality shows started dreaming big, started wanting different lives from the ones they'd lived before.

"I just can't stop thinking about how she was the one to find him," Ricky said, gesturing to the screen. "That kind of thing can ruin a person, haunt them, you know? Do you think that's why she had to get away?"

"Maybe," I said. And maybe finding Franco had been the catalyst for Tess's departure, had given her the opportunity to leave, but Tess turning down Ricky's proposal meant she'd never wanted to stay here forever.

"I just wish he'd never done it. For a lot of reasons," Ricky said, and I nodded.

"Hey!" shouted Bo from the end of the hall. "I'm closing up!"

"Thanks, man," said Ricky. "We're heading out soon."

On the computer another clip of Franco played. He was in Maine now, sitting at a picnic table near the ocean wearing dark sunglasses and eating a lobster roll, his gray curls blowing wildly in the breeze coming in from the water. Franco was sitting across from a younger man, who wore a barn coat and pointed a finger toward the ocean as he, too, ate a lobster roll. Then the screen went black and in the next scene Franco and the man in the barn coat were in a lighthouse. The man showed Franco the switch that turned on the beacon that beamed from top. Then they climbed the spiral staircase and went out onto the catwalk outside the lighthouse. The volume on the computer was still off, so we could hear Bo up front shutting down and locking up while the screen showed Franco talking to the man in the barn coat. Ricky got up and took the sack of doughnuts off the filing cabinet, unfolded the bag, tilted it toward me, and I took one. On the screen Franco stood on the catwalk, one hand shading his face from the sun, the other pointing at the horizon line where water met sky. We sat silently in the back office as Bo shouted good-bye, ate the doughnuts, and watched Franco explore the big, wide world.

ROLAND RACCOON

One

Ms. Gardner had not been in support of the plan to drag Roland Raccoon to every middle school science class, but the principal said they'd paid Margery Martin a flat fee for the school visit and it would be a waste if every student at Galaville Middle School did not have the opportunity to visit with Roland. Ms. Gardner was certain the eighth graders in her sixth-period class were too old to learn life lessons about kindness and compassion and giving everyone and everything a chance from a twelve-year-old blind raccoon that was also deaf in one ear. "But he loves to be sung to," Margery Martin informed the class, adding, "in his good ear." She cradled Roland in her lap as if he were a baby.

Margery leaned down, put her lips disturbingly close to Roland's ear, and sang something that might have been a Frank Sinatra song. The boys who were sitting against a bookshelf near the rear of the classroom, as far away from Margery as they were allowed, snickered, and Ms. Gardner heard the word "rabies" whispered several times. Margery was in her seventies, wore a baggy sweatshirt with a large cartoon raccoon's face on it, pink elastic-waist pants, and thick-soled orthopedic shoes. Perhaps the fifth graders might find something charming in her, might think she was similar in some way to their beloved grandmothers, but the eighth graders were surely too jaded to believe that spending an hour sitting cross-legged on the floor surrounding a woman crooning to a raccoon splayed on her lap was a good use of their time. There were twenty-four of them in a semicircle on the floor. Well, twenty-three of them were cross-legged on the ground; Julia Fredericks was in a wheelchair. During the summer Julia had gone to visit her cousins on Long Island and had been in a boating accident where her legs had been crushed. Doctors were unsure if she would walk again. Some of the girls in the class treated Julia as if she were their wounded pet, making sure to follow her everywhere and offering to help her at all times, even when it was clear she did not need their help. These girls were well-intentioned, even though they were mostly in Julia's way. Julia had been remarkably patient with the girls fussing over her, and Ms. Gardner had thought of nominating Julia for Eighth Grade Student of the Year for this patience and for her resilience in the face of adversity, but she was afraid others would believe Julia's nomination (and likely win) to be the result of teachers feeling sorry for her.

"Many people think I saved Roland's life but, really, he saved mine," Margery said. She then explained that before Roland came into her life her husband had passed away, and she was lonely and very, very depressed. She'd thought her life was no longer worth living. *Was she implying she had been suicidal?* Ms. Gardner wondered. *Was this proper information to disclose to the students?* During her time of great sadness Margery found Roland Raccoon down the street from where she used to live in upstate New York. "I don't live here in New York anymore, though," she said, "because they don't allow you to keep raccoons as pets. Seven years ago I moved to New Hampshire to start a new life with Roland." That last sentence, taken out of context, might indicate a second marriage, a fresh start that didn't include fleeing a state because of its laws about harboring wildlife in one's home. "When I found Roland he was in terrible shape. Some boys had beaten him with a baseball bat."

After that revelation, several of the boys sat up straight and took notice of what Margery was saying. Sam Rizzo sat up especially tall, interest washing over his face. Ms. Gardner worried about Sam; she saw violence bubbling beneath his surface, and every once in a while he could no longer control his emotions and would punch or kick a classmate. She was fairly certain Sam was covertly murdering the crickets the students were supposed to be feeding Lyle, the iguana that lived in the classroom, dropping their crushed bodies in a row on the windowsill. Since she didn't have any solid evidence to prove Sam was the perpetrator, all she could do was quietly sweep the cricket carcasses into the trash can at the end of every school day.

"Oh, poor Roland," said Chloe Trainer. She wobbled side to side on her haunches and put her hands under her butt. Ms. Gardner was certain Chloe sat on her hands so she wouldn't run up and grab Roland out of Margery's arms, hold him to her chest, and try to absorb the pains of his past. Chloe was one of the kindest students Ms. Gardner had ever encountered, and she worried about her almost as much as she worried about Sam Rizzo. Ms. Gardner was unsure if the world was a more inhospitable place for people with tendencies toward violence or extreme kindness.

"Yes, poor Roland," said Margery. She bent down and kissed the raccoon on top of his head, and he wiggled his legs in what Ms. Gardner could only describe as satisfied pleasure. "Poor Mr. Roly Poly." Margery rubbed his belly and his fur ruffled under her hand.

A ripple of snickers passed through the boys again, then Sam raised his hand. "Did Roland get blind because he was beaten?"

"That's right," said Margery. "Beaten and left for dead."

"And then did you have to feed Roland from a bottle?" asked Chloe. Ms. Gardner saw the combination of sympathy and excitement on Chloe's face and knew Chloe was imagining herself bottle-feeding a wounded raccoon, soothing it with clucking sounds, tucking it into a soft bed under fluffy blankets.

"I did feed him with a bottle since he couldn't chew because of his injuries. Although before I got him he was at the animal hospital for over a month and was fed through an I.V. because his jaw was shattered."

"My dad said that when we brought our dog to the animal hospital after he got his paw stung by wasps and it got all swollen up and he had an allergic reaction it cost enough that we couldn't go on vacation," said Phil Steinway, pushing his glasses up his nose. "We were supposed to go to Florida and go to the Wizarding World of Harry Potter, but we didn't."

"Animal care, especially of a special needs animal, is very expensive. This is why I ask for donations when Roly and I come speak at schools."

A "donation," that's what Margery called her fifteen-hundred-dollar fee? No wonder the principal wanted Margery to haul the raccoon around the school. Margery told the students that even though Roland had been left for dead, she'd known he was a fighter, known if he wanted to live badly enough he would, and no matter how much it cost her to bring him into her home, it would be worth it. And now Roland was an important raccoon, she said, maybe even the most important raccoon in all of the world because he taught young people lessons, helped them understand that even if someone was different, they still had love in their hearts and they were still worth loving. Ms. Gardner glanced at Julia in her wheelchair, tried to see what she was making of all this, but Julia just looked blankly at Roland. Ms. Gardner hated the notion of people (and animals, she supposed) getting better because they'd fought a good fight. Sometimes people got ill or injured, and even if they wanted to live or get better, they didn't, no matter how much fight they had in them. Last year her father died. He was fifty-eight. There was a lot more he'd wanted to do with his life, but no matter what he tried—the medications, the experimental trials—nothing worked. It had certainly not been a matter of his not *wanting* to live. Maybe Roland Raccoon was lucky that Margery had swooped into his life and had nursed him to health, but that was because he *could* be nursed. A few more swings of the baseball bat and there would have been no rescuing Roland.

Ms. Gardner noticed most of the students were getting bored with Margery and Roland. Soon they would get distracted and then trouble would start. Here's what she wished she could tell her students when their eyes dimmed, when they deemed school dull: when you grow up, life is boring. Work is tedious. If adults misbehaved every time they got bored, the world would be in a state of chaos. Day after day you do the same thing. Sure, maybe one day a raccoon will show up at your job, but even the raccoon won't be particularly interesting and it will likely create opportunities for people to misbehave and will make your job harder.

Down near the wheels of Julia's wheelchair sat Brianna Merchant looking exceptionally bored, her cheeks resting in both palms, her eyes fluttering closed. In her lap she held a pencil case, which was an odd thing, since they were only listening to Margery, not writing anything in response to her visit yet. Brianna had long, shiny blonde hair and a complexion that glowed smoothly, even though most of her classmates were speckled with pimples. She was one of the girls that other girls wanted to emulate. Girls like Brianna sparked the interest of boys; they were the type that decades later boys would remember as their first unrequited crush. And girls like Brianna knew they could be cruel to the less popular or homely or fidgety nervous boys and there would be no repercussions.

Ms. Gardner was nearly certain Brianna had been the one to cut a hole in the bottom of Richie Detwiler's backpack last week while it rested on the floor. When he'd put it on as class ended, all his books slipped out and everyone laughed. Well, everyone except for Chloe Trainer, who'd immediately leapt from her desk to help Richie collect his books and papers. At first Ms. Gardner had thought the backpack had simply worn out, but then, as the rest of the class was gathering their books, she heard Brianna say to Matilda Chen, "He deserved it since he's always packing up a few minutes early, while Ms. Gardner is still talking. Every single day he packs up early and disrupts the class." Then Ms. Gardner had known that Brianna was culpable in some way for Richie's ruined backpack. It was likely she hadn't cut it herself, that she'd convinced one of her henchwomen—this is how Ms. Gardner had come to think of the girls that trailed Brianna everywhere—to do it.

But now Ms. Gardner watched as Brianna leaned forward, reached out, and stuck a pencil in one of the spokes of Julia's wheelchair. Then she stuck a second pencil in another spoke. What was she doing? And why was she bold enough to do it herself and not employ one of her henchwomen to do her dirty work for her?

Two

For the first two months of the school year, Ms. Gardner had harbored a mild hatred for Brianna. Ms. Gardner knew that had she and Brianna been the same age, some of Brianna's cruelty and disapproval would have been directed her way. By eighth grade Ms. Gardner still had not shed her lisp; it would take four more years and a great deal of hard work with a speech therapist for it to fade. The mean girls at Ms. Gardner's school had ridiculed the lisp, especially after Ms. Gardner won first place in the school's science fair and had to present her project on forensics and the science of fingerprints to the entire school from the stage in the auditorium. Still, over a decade later, she can remember the giggles while she talked about loops, arches, ridges, and whorls in fingerprints, all those s-sounds in all those words slushing in her mouth, the noise of girls giggling in the audience magnified by the acoustics of the auditorium. It was hard not to think of those laughing girls when Ms. Gardner looked at Brianna.

Things turned truly bad between Ms. Gardner and Brianna in November. The week before Thanksgiving, Ms. Gardner had been on a blind date at a Mexican chain restaurant in the mall. Her date, Orion, smelled like a health food store, had longer hair than she did, and looked remarkably like Weird Al. Her father had loved Weird Al, and even though Ms. Gardner was too young to have appreciated his heyday, she'd developed a fondness for his music. Her father had played his Weird Al CDs over and over again when she was a kid, and they'd sung along to "Girls Just Want to Have Lunch" and "Addicted to Spuds," their favorite songs. It wasn't until years later that she realized Weird Al remade other musicians' songs with funny lyrics and a lot of people found him to be ridiculous. Ms. Gardner looked across the table at Orion and puzzled over why he would be wearing a tank top in upstate New York at the end of November. In his tank top, Orion looked like Weird Al on the cover of *Running With Scissors*, where he was sprinting on a track holding up a large pair of scissors in each hand. Thinking of the album cover made her unexpectedly sad, made her miss her father profoundly.

The waitress came by to take their order, and Orion questioned the poor waitress exhaustively about many items on the menu because he was a vegan. Ms. Gardner was angry at her landlord, Mrs. Petronelli, for setting her up on the date with Orion, who was her nephew. When Mrs. Petronelli had suggested the date to Ms. Gardner, she'd asked, "How old are you now? Twenty five?"

"Twenty-four," Ms. Gardner corrected her.

"Well, you don't have forever to find a man. I don't see you ever out with any men since Will moved away. You can't live alone forever."

Ms. Gardner wanted to tell Mrs. Petronelli that *she* also lived alone (unfortunately, on the second floor of Ms. Gardner's duplex, which allowed Mrs. Petronelli to watch Ms. Gardner's comings and goings and allowed Ms. Gardner to hear Mrs. Petronelli's television blasting game shows at all hours of the day and night). Living alone didn't seem to affect Mrs. Petronelli's life of meddling, watching television, and collecting rent on the four duplexes she owned on the block. The only reason she'd even agreed to go on the date was because Mrs. Petronelli had hinted she'd raise Ms. Gardner's rent if she did not.

The waitress came back with their beers, and as Ms. Gardner watched the waitress walk back toward the kitchen, she spotted Brianna Merchant and her mother at a table across the restaurant.

"My student is here," Ms. Gardner whispered.

"What? Where?" barked Orion.

Ms. Gardner fought the urge to lift a finger to her mouth, to shush him the way she shushed Sam Rizzo on a daily basis during class.

"It doesn't matter where," said Ms. Gardner.

"Should we go say hi?"

We, thought Ms. Gardner. *We?!* She could imagine what would happen in school on Monday if she dragged a frizzy-haired, patchouli-scented man named Orion across the restaurant and introduced him to Brianna and her mother. The gossip would be never-ending. "We should just stay put. Could you imagine if you were in eighth grade and out with your family and a teacher came over to talk to you? Wouldn't you have been mortified?" She thought then of Will, who'd broken up with her last fall when he'd gone across the country to start a PhD in physics at Berkeley. They'd been together for five years, through most of college and then the just-starting-out years afterward, and then he was gone, out of her life. He'd said their relationship would be impossible to sustain with over three thousand miles between them. She hated him for believing that and tried not to have any fond thoughts about him, but Will would have understood her need to hide from Brianna. He'd have ducked under the table with her, would have pretended to be searching for a dropped fork or a lost earring; he would have hidden under the table with her until Brianna was gone.

"I think it would be nice as a student to see a teacher in a social context," said Orion.

"No," said Ms. Gardner because she didn't want to explain how profoundly weird it was to see students outside of school. Again, she used the tone she had to trot out when dealing with Sam Rizzo. *No, don't touch the Bunsen burners. No, do not clang the test tubes against each other. No, don't even make jokes about weighing drugs on the laboratory scales.* Ms. Gardner knew her students were intrigued by what her life was like outside of the classroom because she was younger than all the other teachers on her teaching team, yet when she encountered students outside of school, they were strange and awkward. Last week she'd seen Celia Nemer in the bathroom at the movie theater. After Celia washed her hands and turned around to look for the paper towel dispenser and saw Ms. Gardner coming out of a stall, Celia's mouth dropped and she stared, wordless, water dripping from her fingers. Ms. Gardner felt as if she'd been caught doing something wrong, but she'd only been doing something human, peeing, after consuming thirty-two ounces of Diet Coke.

"It's nice to see you, Celia," Ms. Gardner said. But it had not been nice to see Celia. The truth was she was at the movies alone, and if Celia found out that Ms. Gardner was so pathetic as to not be able to even scrape up one friend to see a movie with, that bit of gossip would be spread to all of Celia's friends. Celia was one of Brianna's henchwomen, and once Brianna heard about Ms. Gardner's pathetic friendlessness the whole grade would know. But Ms. Gardner *had* had a movie buddy until quite recently. Since graduating college she and her friend Emily had seen a movie every Wednesday. Ms. Gardner would rush out of school as soon as the final bell rang, telling the other teachers on her team that she had a standing appointment on Wednesday afternoons. She suspected the others thought she was being cagey because she was going to therapy, and because of this they never questioned her Wednesday afternoon activities. Emily worked at Starbucks for the two years after graduation, and she, too, told her employer that she could not work on Wednesday afternoons because of an important weekly engagement. And so every Wednesday they'd see a movie together. It didn't matter if it was a good movie or a bad one, if it featured aliens or monsters or a love story, or if it took place centuries ago or in the future. They just liked the escape of the cool, dark theater the popcorn-scented air, falling into the world of the movie and not having to worry about money or jobs or their social lives for a few hours. But this fall Emily quit her job at Starbucks and took on a full-time job as a live-in nanny for a rich family, and her Wednesday afternoons were no longer free. On the two evenings a week she was free she was too tired for the movies. So Ms. Gardner now went to the movies alone on Wednesdays because she didn't have to supervise any Wednesday after-school activities and didn't want to go home and listen to Mrs. Petronelli's blaring television while sitting alone in her apartment. She'd have to figure out how to hide the fact that she was at the theater alone from Celia, but after a few moments of staring, Celia said her friend was waiting outside the bathroom so she had to leave *immediately*. Celia sprinted out of the bathroom, crashing into a woman rooting around in an enormous purse, sending the tube of lipstick the woman had been holding flying, and nearly knocking the woman over.

Now, cheeseless, meatless, sour cream-less nachos were delivered to Orion, and a burger was placed in front of Ms. Gardner. Ms. Gardner took a large bite of her Olé Burger and bloody meat juice dribbled from her burger to her plate. To his credit, Orion did not seem to be judging her food. Orion talked about his job at a store that sold running gear, and Ms. Gardner halfway listened to his stories about customers who came into the store to get their gaits analyzed and their shoes professionally fitted and then declared they'd buy the shoes Orion recommended for a better price online, but her attention was focused on Brianna. Soon after a waitress brought drinks to Brianna and her mother, a bartender came around the bar and joined them at their table. He was handsome in the way of men who'd been popular athletes in high school—good bone structure, wide shoulders, a confident way of moving—and looked to be at least a decade younger than Brianna's mother. Ms. Gardner knew about Brianna's parents' acrimonious divorce and had been warned by the vice principal that Brianna might exhibit some behavioral issues as a result. There was a great deal of money and property involved, allegations of infidelity, and rumors of Brianna's mother intentionally crashing her father's Mercedes into the garage of the woman with whom her father was purportedly having an affair. As soon as the bartender sat down, Brianna's mother's attention shifted fully to him. At one point Brianna picked up her mother's drink—something pink in a martini glass—and drained it and looked longingly at her mother, who was still not paying any attention to her. As soon as Brianna finished her quesadilla, her mother gave Brianna a credit card and shooed her away, likely urging her to go into the mall so she and the bartender could have some time alone. Brianna stood lingering at the edge of the table, staring at her mother, but her mother waved Brianna away again. Brianna walked toward the door and Ms. Gardner hunched down in her seat. Brianna looked at her feet as she walked, and Ms. Gardner thought she was safe. After all, she'd sent Celia Nemer sprinting out of the women's room at the movie theater; even a student as confident and bold as Brianna certainly wouldn't seek out a teacher outside of school. Ms. Gardner pretended to rearrange her napkin again and again in her lap, trying to look busy. It was clear that Brianna felt powerful at school, surrounded by her henchwomen, but here, with her mother, the dynamics had shifted. Ms. Garner knew she should feel sympathy toward Brianna, but she did not. Ms. Gardner's eyes were still affixed to the napkin in her lap when she heard Orion cough in a dramatic fashion in order to get her attention. She looked up and saw Brianna standing by their table, her mother's credit card flitting between her hands.

"Hi, Ms. Gardner." Brianna grinned as though she now knew an enormous and incriminating secret.

"Brianna!" said Ms. Gardner. She balled up her napkin and continued to squeeze it while Brianna looked back-and-forth between Ms. Gardner and Orion. "What a surprise to see you here."

"Is this your husband?" said Brianna. Ms. Gardner wished desperately that Will was sitting across from her. Will with his short, neat haircut and round tortoiseshell glasses and checked shirts. Will, who looked so normal.

"I'm her friend," said Orion, extending his hand to Brianna. She looked puzzled about the extended hand, then shook it after a long pause. "My name is Orion."

"Ohhh," said Brianna, dragging out the word and staring at him for several moments longer than would be deemed polite. "Like the constellation."

"Precisely," said Orion. "Great job making that connection!" He held his hand up for a high five, and Brianna reluctantly brought her hand up to slap his. Ms. Gardner felt a swell of panic. She sensed they were only moments away from Orion inviting Brianna to join them for the rest of dinner.

"Are you a teacher too?" said Brianna. Ms. Gardner smelled alcohol on Brianna's breath.

"No, I'm training for marathons and work at The Runner's Edge, selling running gear."

"Oh," said Brianna. She was clearly unimpressed.

"And you're in Mia's class?"

Brianna paused. Orion had used Ms. Gardner's first name. Of course Ms. Gardner's students knew she had a first name but she didn't know if it had ever been spoken aloud in their presence.

"Yes. Sixth period physical science," said Brianna.

"What a special surprise it is to meet one of Mia's students," said Orion.

"Well," said Ms. Gardner, putting a hand on Brianna's shoulder. It felt thin and boney under her hand. She rarely touched her students, but right now she wanted to turn Brianna around, shove her hard on the back, push her toward the restaurant's exit. "We don't want to keep you. You go enjoy the mall."

"Want a nacho?" said Orion, holding up a chip coated in refried beans and guacamole.

Brianna stepped back from the chip, held at her eye level. "I should go," she said. "See you Monday, Ms. Gardner."

Monday, of course, went as expected. There were knowing looks, whispers, and giggles all through the classroom. Ms. Gardner was not being paranoid; they were all talking about her, laughing at her, and although she was the one with the dry-erase markers and the grade book, she felt thirteen again. After Ms. Gardner took attendance, Brianna's hand shot up. "Are we going to do a unit on astronomy this year?" she asked. "I'm especially interested in learning all about the constellations." Her henchwomen snickered.

"Astronomy isn't currently part of the eighth grade curriculum," Ms. Gardner said, trying to make her words as curt as possible. But it was too late. Now all had been revealed about her: she had a first name, she peed, and she was passionately in love with a frizzy-haired, tank-top-wearing man named Orion. There was little chance she could come back from all of this.

Three

"Do you know what Roland's favorite activity is?" asked Margery. "It's dancing! Could you?" she said, turning to Ms. Gardner, and pointing to a battery-powered tape player she'd brought to class in a canvas tote bag. Ms. Gardner wondered how many of her students had ever seen a tape player before. To them, the tape player might seem more exotic than the raccoon, something more worthy of scientific study. Ms. Gardner pushed the play button and polka music filled the room. Ms. Gardner's knowledge of polka music stemmed entirely from Weird Al's polka songs, and hearing the music made her think of that awful date with Orion three months before. Things had not been the same in her classroom since Brianna came back and squealed to everyone about him; Ms. Gardner had felt her authority slipping out of her hands after that weekend. Margery stood up, placed Roland on the ground, held his front paws, and they danced together, Roland taking tiny steps and keeping pace with Margery's movements. "Join us!" Margery shouted to the class, but everyone sat still, staring at Margery and Roland.

"My grandpa plays this kind of music! He has tapes too," said Zach Goss excitedly as he stood up. "Last summer when I visited him we went to the Austrian Community Center and I learned how to do a folk dance."

"Would you teach us all how?" Margery said, clearly delighted, and Zach nodded. Poor, earnest, kind Zach, with his crisply ironed tucked-in shirts and polished black leather shoes and neatly gelled hair, who clearly did not see how this dancing was not a good idea. Zach held up his arms in demonstration, and still no one moved.

"Get up, everyone," said Ms. Gardner. "*Now*," she added sharply. That extra syllable seemed to have a magic effect on the students, who sprang to their feet. Oh, but there was Julia Fredericks in her wheelchair, and she obviously could not "get up" as Ms. Gardner had ordered, and Ms. Gardner was furious with herself for her choice of words since Julia could still move her body in her wheelchair, do some approximation of Margery and Zach's dance. Why hadn't she just said, "Dance!"? But here was Chloe Trainer, already up on her feet, her hands extended to Julia. And here was Julia taking Chloe's hands in hers, smiling. And here was Brianna, still on the ground, her pencil case open, sticking more pencils into the spokes of Julia's wheelchair. Ms. Gardner pounced, clasping Brianna's hands in one of hers, pulling the pencils out of Julia's wheel, throwing them to a corner of the room, grabbing Brianna's pencil case, pushing it hard so it glided all the way to the wall. "What are you doing?" said Brianna, and Ms. Gardner pulled Brianna to her feet. "Don't be an asshole," Ms. Gardner whispered. "Were you trying to break her wheelchair?" Brianna's eyes widened. Ms. Gardner knew she shouldn't call a student an asshole, but what other word was there for Brianna? Children with other problems—distraction, hyperactivity, overly talkative, daydreamers—could change, but Brianna was mean, and meanness was something that lasted one's entire life. It was not something that could be shed like a snake's skin once a person reached maturity. "Dance with me," ordered Ms. Gardner, because what worse indignity could a thirteen-year-old suffer than having to dance with her teacher in front of all her classmates? Ms. Gardner held Brianna's hands and pulled her far from Julia and Chloe, who were moving just a little bit to the beat of the polka music, who were not following Zach's directions, but who looked lovely and happy dancing together, Julia in her wheelchair and Chloe gliding from side to side in front of Julia, and Ms. Gardner swore she would scream at any child who dared utter a word about Julia and Chloe dancing together being "gay."

"Do exactly as Zach says," Ms. Gardner ordered. She wanted Brianna humiliated, like she'd been the Monday after her date with Orion. Ms. Gardner had nothing to lose, had already been laughed at and talked about in this classroom for three months, but Brianna had everything to lose by not being her usual cold, composed, in-control self. Ms. Gardner expected Brianna to argue, to refuse to dance with her, but Brianna followed Zach's instructions, raising her arms, lifting her feet.

"Just follow the oom-paa-paa," said Zach, and the room filled with more giggles. The only people who weren't laughing and who were dancing sincerely were Ms. Gardner and Brianna, Chloe and Julia, and Margery and Roland Raccoon, who had closed his blind eyes and was now gently swaying side to side with Margery as if they were smitten teenagers at a school dance.

"When the song ends and we're done dancing, I'll sit back down with Roly in my lap, and then anyone who wants to can line up and pet him gently," said Margery. "Roly is good luck, and if you pet him and whisper your hopes and wishes into his good ear, he might make them come true."

"Can I?" said Brianna quietly.

"Can you touch the raccoon?" said Ms. Gardner.

Brianna nodded. For the first time in the classroom that year Brianna's cold facade had fallen away. Ms. Gardner recognized the expression on her face from that day at the restaurant in the mall, the way Brianna had looked at her mother, seeming vulnerable and needy. It was stranger, though, to see Brianna looking vulnerable in a classroom, in *Ms. Gardner's classroom*.

"I suppose you can pet him," said Ms. Gardner. She'd actually thought of *making* Brianna touch Roland, thought of punishing her by forcing her to touch the old, blind, half-deaf raccoon, which seemed like the kind of creature Brianna would not want to be near.

As the music ended Zach took a deep bow, which triggered another surge of laughter throughout the classroom. "What a talented young man!" Margery declared, then she took Roland's paws and made him clap for Zach. "Roland says thank you."

"You are very welcome, Roland," said Zach, and he bowed again in the raccoon's direction.

"You can be the first to pet Roly," said Margery, as she settled back in her chair and hefted Roland onto her lap. Zach smiled and ran his hand down Roland's back, then rubbed his ears, and Ms. Gardner could have sworn that Roland's mouth shifted into a small smile.

"Anyone else who wants to pet Roland should get in line behind Zach," said Ms. Gardner. "And you're last in line," she said to Brianna.

Brianna trudged to the end of the line, and again Ms. Gardner was surprised she didn't argue. After Zach petted Roland he moved away, back to his desk. Then Chloe and Julia both petted Roland, and Margery even let Roland sit in Julia's lap for a minute. Roland stood and wrapped his front legs around Julia's neck in a hug, which made Julia laugh, and Ms. Gardner was glad Julia got to do something special. As he waited impatiently in line for Julia to finish with Roland, Sam Rizzo let out an enormous, resonating burp, and Ms. Gardner told him that since he could not behave himself he could not pet Roland. "I didn't want rabies anyway!" he shouted as he stormed to his seat. Most of the students wanted a chance to pet Roland, but none of them whispered anything into his ear. They'd be made fun of if their classmates saw them whispering to a raccoon. If any of them still secretly believed in luck, they could do quiet, private things like look up to the night sky and silently wish on a star or keep a lucky penny in their pocket on test days.

Ms. Gardner longed for the days when she still believed in the power of someone or something to grant wishes. If she believed in Roland's ability to make wishes come true, she'd wish for her father to still be alive, to be well and happy, listening to silly songs with her. She'd wish for Will to still be here with her, not across the country holed up in a lab, maybe missing her, maybe not. And if she were allowed a third small wish, she'd wish Emily was still available for Wednesday movies. If she could push it to four wishes, she'd wish she were better at her job. The science was not the issue—she'd always excelled in school, had been good at experiments and hypotheses, patient with lab work during college—but it was dealing with these kids, not calling them assholes, not slipping up and telling a student in a wheelchair to get up, not resenting them as though they were the same kids who'd mocked and hurt her more than ten years ago, that was difficult.

It was finally Brianna's turn. Ms. Gardner thought about the pencils stuck in the spokes of Julia's wheels, let her eyes dart to where they were still on the floor in the corner of the classroom. She suspected Brianna might pull Roland's tail or squeeze his head or poke one of his foggy eyes. Her body tensed and she prepared to spring forward, to grab Brianna and pull her away from Roland. Brianna reached out a hand, touched Roland's head gently, then lowered herself to her knees, her lips nearly touching the raccoon's ear, her gaze focused on Roland's unseeing eyes, ignoring the rest of the class, who had stopped their moving and rustling and fidgeting and were all staring at her. It was so silent in the classroom that everyone could hear even the quietest sounds, and Ms. Gardner was stunned and surprised when Brianna whispered, right there in front of everyone, "Roland? Can you help me? I have things I need to tell you."

VANISHED

I had good reasons for not liking Hayley at first. Seven minutes after we received an email from our college's Residential Life Office informing us we would be roommates, she sent me an enthusiastic email. This indicated Hayley had nothing better to do than wait for my contact information and pounce on it. Her eagerness was overwhelming. I wondered whether she'd always be so demanding of my attention as we spent the year forced to room together. I had planned to let the email from Residential Life marinate for two weeks or so before reaching out. I didn't want to seem too eager. Eagerness indicates that you care, and caring means that, inevitably, you'll be hurt.

But it was not only the fact that she had sent an email so quickly that bothered me; the sign-off on the email was also questionable. She signed off with "Ciao." *Ciao*, as if she were a beautiful Italian woman mouthing the word as she waved from a train to her lover on the platform while the train pulled away from the station in Milan. I reread her email after I came to the unfortunate sign-off and saw she was from a town called Rome, New York, and this made me wonder for a brief moment if perhaps it was not such an egregious transgression to sign off with *ciao* if one was from a Rome of any sort.

Upon reflection, I shouldn't have been so upset about the *ciao*. There were worse sign-offs. Once I got to college I noticed almost every professor signed off their emails with "Best." "Best *what*?" I always wanted to ask. Best in show? Best pumpkin grown in the state of New York? Best Western? I suppose it was short for "Best wishes," but would it take so much extra effort to write the word "wishes"? At least *ciao* meant something, just that one word.

After receiving her email, I decided to research Hayley Totorelli from Rome, New York, to see what I could find on the Internet. I was busy trying to discern whether Totorelli was an Italian last name because if it was then maybe there would be a bit more validity to her signing off emails with *ciao*. Maybe she was even a recent immigrant from Italy, although I doubted it since that would probably be something she would have mentioned in her exhaustive introductory email. While I was snooping on her, a Facebook friend request arrived from, of course, Hayley Totorelli from Rome, New York. No one our age used Facebook anymore; now it was just a place for grandmas to wish people happy birthday, so I wondered whether Hayley was someone who was eighteen yet acted like some old lady. Would she bark at me to put on a jacket every time I departed our room? Would she ask me if I was drinking enough water every day? I felt gross about snooping on her while she had reached out to me twice, but not gross enough to respond immediately. I would let the friend request sit for a few days. I knew that people who accepted immediately were considered losers with nothing better to do. I also believed I was supposed to wait a few days to answer emails because this made one seem busy and important. Trust me, this wasn't my own theory. I read about it in the *New York Times*, in an article about making yourself seem important by being scarce in these times of constant connectivity.

Let us fast forward a few weeks into my freshman year. At first Hayley and I were friends, or whatever it is you call someone who sleeps every night in the same room you do and who eats all their meals in the dining hall with you. I don't think it would be wrong to use the word friends to describe what we were. Everyone on our hall fell into a sort of clump of friendship, traveling together like a herd of under-rested, overcaffeinated sheep. Everyone seemed to assume Residential Life had done a good job of matching people as roommates and gravitated most to the person or two people they had been assigned to room with. I would not say I filled out my roommate interest form with much seriousness or honesty. For my hobbies I put down camping, acting, art, and politics because I thought if someone did happen to glance at this form, they would approve of the breadth of my interests.

But here is the truth: I thought camping would make me seem outdoorsy and active without actually committing myself to a particular sport. God forbid the field hockey coach or the tennis coach came knocking if I falsely put down one of those sports as an interest. I jogged almost every day, but that was just to clear my mind of the anxious thoughts that swirled endlessly and annoyingly around it. I certainly didn't want to participate in cross-country or track in any formal way. I had been camping once in my life, with the Brownies, right before I quit the troop. A crow appeared early in the morning and poked its sharp beak into the side of my tent like some deranged psycho with a pickax, and that was enough for me to quit camping forever. I liked mindlessly watching shows on Netflix, binging one episode after the next, but I had never stepped on a stage as an actor. I did not act, unless you count the facade that each and every one of us must put on when we leave our homes each morning. I did like to doodle in the margins of my notebooks, but I wouldn't consider myself an artist in any way. As for politics, I was mildly interested, but I perceived it more as a spectator sport than something to get my body and soul involved in.

It turned out, however, that Hayley was actually interested in three of the four categories I put down on the roommate form— camping, acting, and politics—and these activities guided her toward clubs and people outside of our clump of freshmen who lived on the same floor of the same dorm. Throughout the fall Hayley would go off on the bus with some activist friends to protests in the city, marching against police brutality and marching for equal rights, and marching against the president. She knew at eighteen who she was and what she stood for. I was still trying to figure things out; I was not yet someone with strong convictions.

Each time Hayley put on her hiking boots and picked up one of the poster board signs she'd worked on with a vast array of markers, she'd say, "Hey, Margaret, you want to come?" and I'd always tell her I was too busy and had too much homework to do. I believed in the same things Hayley believed in, but couldn't a person believe in things without proclaiming them publicly? Couldn't one believe in something *quietly*? I couldn't tell if Hayley was disappointed in me when I kept telling her no, but I was afraid of getting hurt or getting arrested at a protest or having my picture appear in the newspaper and having my parents—who have very conservative values—see it and say they would no longer pay for college because it was turning me into a liberal snowflake. I knew they'd use this term because they said it five years earlier about my older sister, who wanted to switch from pre-med to an English major during her sophomore year. They said they were not paying hundreds of thousands of dollars for her to read novels all day and if she wanted to read books she could do it on the beach during her vacations after she became a surgeon. I had not yet declared a major; my parents thought economics would be good for me because I was quick with numbers, but I didn't know if that's what I wanted to major in. Hayley had already declared a theater major, and that was yet another sign of her certainty, of knowing who she was and what she wanted to pursue.

By the time Halloween rolled around, our hall group had begun to go in separate directions, with most people finding friends and people to date in classes and clubs and sometimes at parties, leaving only a few losers behind. I suppose I should say I was part of this loser group even though I did not and still do not consider myself a loser.

I think there's a great deal of difference between being a loser and a loner, even though those two words have four letters in common.

Instead of going home to Rome, New York, for Thanksgiving, Hayley decided to stay on campus and spend Thanksgiving serving food to the homeless and otherwise unfortunate at a shelter downtown. "You could come home with me," I told her, after I heard her Thanksgiving plans. I didn't particularly want her to see my home and to realize my family was well off, and to assume maybe I didn't go to protests with her because I was out of touch with the common man. I didn't want to subject her to my mother's strict rules about the correct fork to use for each course and the proper glass to use for each type of beverage, but I did want my parents to meet Hayley. I wanted them to see I was capable of making a friend. Throughout my childhood, they'd spent a great deal of time fretting about my not being social enough, not ever wanting to invite other children over to my house to play, and never receiving invitations to other people's houses.

"That's super nice of you to offer," said Hayley, "but I'll be fine here. Do you know they make a special Thanksgiving dinner in the dining hall? I think it's mostly for international students, but it'll be kind of fun to be on the campus when it's mostly quiet, you know?"

I nodded and for a moment debated asking Hayley if I could stay here on campus in our room with her, but I knew my parents would be upset if I didn't come home. Instead, I said, "Would international students even care about Thanksgiving?"

Hayley looked like she was going to say something, but she just shook her head. Then she said, "I'm going camping on Friday and Saturday. I'm allowed to use all the camping equipment for free because I joined the Outdoors Club. You know Cassie and Linds? They're going with me."

"Do people camp at Thanksgiving? I thought that was more of a summer activity." I did know Cassie and Linds. They were sophomores and were both sporty—they were on the ultimate frisbee team—and both wore their thick and shiny hair in high ponytails near the top of their heads and seemed to exude good health and sturdiness, much like prized racehorses.

"It's actually going to be kind of warm for this time of the year. And the Outdoors Club has these four-season sleeping bags, so we'll be fine," Hayley said. "It's global warming, and I know I should be upset about it, but I'm kind of happy about no snowstorms over break."

"Where are you going?"

"Linds knows a spot in the Adirondacks she used to go to with her family. She says it should be pretty quiet because tourists don't usually camp there."

I debated telling Hayley the story about the crow ripping through my Brownies tent with its beak but I felt certain she would think it was a weird story that I'd made up to give myself an excuse to quit Brownies, so I didn't tell her. "I'll bring you back some pie," I said. "Do you like pumpkin pie? We usually have pecan too."

Hayley smiled. "That's so nice of you. I would love some pie."

"I could get a big Tupperware container and fill it with all sorts of leftovers. We could have another Thanksgiving here on Sunday night when I get back. I'll bring a little of everything. Dark meat or white?"

"What?" said Hayley, as if she had no idea turkey was a traditional part of the Thanksgiving meal.

"Turkey?"

"Oh, I haven't eaten meat in over a month. We watched this movie about factory farming in my First Year Seminar and it kind of turned me off to meat. You would not believe the conditions some chickens have to live in."

"I didn't know that," I said. And then to clarify I added, "Not the chicken stuff. That I did know. About you being a vegetarian."

"Yeah, I didn't want to go around announcing it. I know how annoying people can be about that kind of thing. I just didn't want to make anyone feel bad for eating meat because it's an individual choice."

"Right," I said. And then I realized it had been over a month since Hayley and I had eaten together, and that's why I didn't know she'd become a vegetarian.

"But pie," Hayley said, "pie would be amazing."

I came back to campus on the Sunday night after Thanksgiving with bags full of food. I planned to say my mother had cooked it all, although she always hired caterers to make our holiday meals, the workers in black pants and crisply ironed white shirts bustling in our kitchen from early morning until the guests arrived at dinnertime. I brought back one container filled with turkey for myself, but as I was walking into the dorm I threw it away in the black iron garbage can outside. There was something grotesque, I thought, about eating turkey in a small enclosed space with a vegetarian looking on, with the scent of cooked turkey flesh wafting through the air. I could tell Hayley the turkey was free range—my mother insisted on ethically raised poultry—but I didn't know if that would help. It was still the flesh of something that had once been living. I toted sweet potato casserole; chestnut stuffing; brussels sprouts; honey-glazed carrots; roasted garlic mashed potatoes; green beans, as they were called in the dining hall, haricot verts, as my mother called them; and an assortment of pie slices. Once they were finished serving my family and our guests, the caterers had packed everything in black plastic takeout containers with clear tops so one could look inside without having to paw the container open. The small refrigerator in our dorm room would not accommodate all this food, but I could deposit what we did not eat in the communal refrigerator down the hall.

When I arrived at our room there was no sliver of light below the door. I had imagined Hayley eagerly waiting for me, excited to see what I'd brought back for her. I set down the bags of food and twisted my backpack around to get my room key from its small outer pocket. The room was cold and empty. Hayley's backpack was missing from the spot where it usually rested, leaning up against her desk. I opened her closet and saw her hiking boots were gone. I thought it strange that Hayley had not returned yet. She was supposed to be back on campus that morning. I pulled out my phone to see if she had texted me, but she hadn't. After the first few weeks of the semester, Hayley had stopped telling me where she'd be, but each night she returned to our shared room, no matter where she'd been earlier.

I busied myself trying to fit as many of the plastic containers into our small refrigerator as I could, stacking them in inventive ways. Despite my efforts, there wasn't enough room for it all, so I kept the pie slices in there and then spent a great deal of time wrapping the rest of the containers with enough masking tape to make it difficult if anyone wanted to steal any of my food. I then wrote my name in Sharpie on the tape and added "You touch, you die," although I now certainly regret writing that. But after a few months of communal living in a dorm, where things—small things, usually, like a favorite pen from the study lounge or a nicely worn-in T-shirt from the laundry room—disappear, I believe the urge to mark one's property like a urinating dog should be forgiven.

By Monday morning Hayley had not returned, nor had she responded to the two texts I'd sent her late Sunday night. I knew she had biology at 9:00 a.m. on Mondays, and her biology textbook and notebook sat, untouched, on her desk. I picked up my phone and scrolled through her Instagram, but she hadn't posted during the past week. I wondered whether she was still in the mountains, whether her phone had no reception wherever she was. My mind went to worst-case scenarios. I thought of a hungry bear, fattening itself before hibernating for the winter, delighted that three delicious-looking people had wandered into the forest. I thought of a car crash and imagined the three of them unconscious on the side of the road. And then I imagined them in a hospital, the machines keeping them alive beeping loudly. I thought maybe their families already knew their fates but I had been kept in the dark because, after all, what was I to Hayley? I was just a roommate who Residential Life had paired with her.

I decided I was being melodramatic. The most likely scenario was that Hayley had returned from camping on Sunday morning and decided she missed being home for Thanksgiving and took a quick jaunt back to Rome. Maybe she'd had breakfast in the dining hall with some international students who were actually from Italy and realized that although those students could not make a trip back to their Rome before classes started up, she could go to her Rome and come back without missing too much school. She would probably return later in the day. I knew she had an A average in biology so she could afford to skip a class.

I wrote her a note, told her there was vegetarian food in the communal fridge and that, of course, I didn't mean *her* when I warned people not to touch the food, and she should help herself. I felt happy in that moment, imagining Hayley returning and finding our small refrigerator filled with pie, and then learning I'd brought even more food back for her and thinking I was a great roommate and maybe even considering living with me again next year, when we had the chance to actually choose the person we wanted to live with. I was in a happy mood and was tempted to sign off my letter with *ciao*, just as a little joke, a reminder of that first email Hayley sent me. But I didn't and just signed my name, even though that was unnecessary since no one else would be leaving her a note on her bed in our room. And now I'm glad I restrained myself from that jokey *ciao* because a few hours later Hayley made her way back to our room in dirty clothes, with unwashed hair, and told me that on Saturday morning she'd discovered two dead women not far from where she, Cassie, and Linds had set up their tent.

Hayley talked and talked, and I realized it had been a long time since we'd spoken more than a few words at a time to each other.

She told me it took them a while to depart on Friday because the president of the Outdoors Club had left campus and forgot to leave them the key for the closet where the camping equipment was stored, so they had to search all over campus for someone from Facilities who could unlock the door, and by the time they reached the area where they wanted to camp it was almost dark. They quickly set up their one large tent they'd chosen over three separate, smaller tents. Then they made a fire and roasted vegetarian hot dogs and then vegetarian marshmallows for s'mores. After eating they cleaned up the food, not wanting to attract bears, and checked to make sure their cooler with hash browns and eggs and pancake mix for breakfast was tightly sealed in the trunk of the old Volvo Linds's parents had given her. There was a lot of back and forth into and out of the car, with getting camping equipment out and sleeping bags and backpacks and the food and cooking supplies moved out of and back into the trunk, and with all that they forgot to lock the car.

None of them heard anything during the night, but when they woke up in the morning the Volvo was gone. They laughed, then, because they were certain it wasn't gone, that maybe they'd just gotten turned around somehow in the dark and the car was farther from the campsite than they thought. I wondered whether they'd been drinking, whether they couldn't remember things because they were hung over and had parked the car drunk the night before.

Hayley said, "I couldn't believe someone was able to hotwire the car without any of us hearing. Linds still had the keys. They were in the pocket of her jeans in the morning."

"Were you wearing your SleepPhones?" I asked, and Hayley nodded. She could not sleep with any noise or light, so she wrapped her head up with these Bluetooth headphones that looked like a fuzzy purple headband and then put on a black eye mask. She could neither see nor hear anything beyond whatever was playing on her phone when she had her nighttime getup on.

"But Cassie and Linds weren't listening to anything and they didn't hear the car start. How is that possible? If I'd been paying attention, maybe I could have stopped whoever did it."

She told me she was the one who'd first seen the bodies. She and Cassie and Linds had been laughing and walking around, thinking the car had to be somewhere nearby and somehow they just weren't seeing it. Linds made a joke about a bear driving it away and they all laughed. They were only a few feet away from their tent when Hayley saw something in the tall, yellowed grass. She screamed and then Cassie and Linds saw what she was screaming about and they screamed too. Then they worried that whoever had killed the two women and had dumped them in the grass was still nearby and could hear them, but then Cassie said, "Someone took the Volvo. We didn't lose it," and they all realized she was right. They were not idiots; they would not lose a three-thousand-pound car.

When Hayley first told me what had happened, I didn't know the murderer was likely the same person who'd killed two other women that year; one woman's body had been found in the Catskills and the other in the Helderbergs. I'd heard about those two cases, but the local news didn't make a big deal of them, and no one talked about the two murders being connected. No one had been afraid to camp and hike, and that's why Hayley, Cassie, and Linds thought camping was a perfect way to spend the break. But after Hayley's discovery, the police announced the three cases might be connected and they warned that campers upstate should be careful.

"I feel like I should have done something," Hayley said.

"How would you have stopped this person?" I asked. "I think if you'd tried they would have hurt you." Whoever this person was had to be strong if they could haul around two bodies, and they had to be quick and smart if they figured out how to steal Linds's car without anyone hearing. They had to be daring, too, to dump the bodies so close to where campers were. It was a cruel and psychotic thing to do; the murderer must have known the campers would find the bodies, and maybe it gave this person a thrill knowing they could damage so many lives in such a short span of time.

"I just feel guilty. Like, why am I still alive when those women aren't? It could have easily been us," said Hayley, as she sat on the bed and bent to take her boots off. "Why were we spared? It just makes the whole world feel so unsafe and dangerous."

"You should take a shower," I said. "You'll feel better after you take a shower." I didn't know what else to say, didn't know how to comfort her.

Hayley nodded, but then she said, "I don't know if I'll ever feel better." She rolled her socks off her feet, slipped on her flip-flops, and grabbed her terrycloth robe from the hook on the side of our tall bookshelf. Then she sat down heavily in her desk chair, the robe draped over her lap.

"How did you get back to campus?"

"We decided to pack up our all our stuff and go. But we all took photos of the bodies so we'd have proof in case something happened to them before we could talk to the police."

I wondered if the photos were still on her phone, but of course I knew I shouldn't ask if they were.

"Then we walked for hours, but we had no idea where we were since we had no reception and GPS wasn't working on our phones. We just walked and walked, and I thought we were going to have to sleep in the woods for another night, but then finally we found a paved road and checked our phones and had reception again, even though by then we all barely had any power left."

Cassie called 911 and reported the bodies. The police came and they all piled into a squad car and Linds remembered the name of the area where they'd camped and they found their way back and the girls sat in the car while the police checked the site. The bodies were gone, and this made all three of them wonder whether the killer had returned and moved them. Or maybe animals had gotten to them. Or maybe the women hadn't been dead at all; maybe, somehow, they'd been pretending, and they'd gotten up and walked away. It felt surreal, Hayley said, her head filled with a swimmy feeling, like she couldn't quite focus on what was right outside the windows of the police cruiser.

"You're lucky, girls," one cop said. "Really lucky."

Hayley, Cassie, and Linds looked out the windows of the car and all wondered if they'd brought the police back to the right spot. They showed the police the photos on their phones and agreed to send them along once there was reception again. The police looked closely at the photographs and identified several trees in the background that looked similar to trees close to where they were. Then they found sticks whose ends were covered in something sticky. A female cop held up one of the sticks, smelled it, then said, "You girls make s'mores?" Yes, they all said, and then they couldn't deny they were in the right spot. "Amazing," said the cop, "amazing how human bodies could just vanish."

Later, I found out that Hayley had returned to campus on Saturday night but felt too upset to come back to our room and stayed for two nights in Cassie and Linds's room, a spacious sophomore double in Bower Hall. I learned this on Tuesday morning, after Hayley spent a sleepless night in our room. She got up and packed a suitcase with most of her clothes and toiletries and then shoved all the books she needed for her classes into her backpack.

"Are you going home early for break?" I asked. There was only a week of classes left before winter break, and then there were exams, and I assumed the school would allow Hayley to make arrangements to finish up at home in light of what she'd experienced.

Hayley shook her head. "I'm just going to move in with Cassie and Linds for the rest of the semester."

"Why?" I said. "Do you want me to clean out the fridge?"

"No, what?"

"There's still all that pie in there." We hadn't eaten any of the Thanksgiving leftovers, and I noticed Hayley had purchased a box of Diet Cokes and couldn't put them in the fridge, so all those cans still sat near the foot of her bed. "I know I left all that pie in there."

Hayley looked confused, then shook her head again. I didn't see any recognition in her eyes, and I wondered if she even remembered the conversation we'd had about pie before break.

"I can clean up the room," I said, although as I looked around I saw that things weren't messy at all.

"It's not that," said Hayley. "It's just that it's weird to be in my own head right now, and I feel like Cassie and Linds are the only people who get it."

I certainly understood how it could feel weird to be in one's own head, but I didn't think Hayley would believe me if I said so. "So are you just going to live with them forever?" I knew I said it in a snappy way, but I felt betrayed. Hadn't I tried to be a good roommate? Hadn't I brought back vegetarian food for our post-Thanksgiving roommate celebration? Hadn't I kept our room clean?

"I don't know," said Hayley. "I just want to be with people who understand."

And that was it. The semester ended and we took our exams and then everyone scattered. I hated being home. I spent most days in my room on my laptop seeing what I could find out about the murdered women and the search for their killer. I learned the women were sisters from Westchester, one a lawyer, the other an engineer, on a weekend girls' retreat in a cabin in the mountains, and they were thirty-eight and forty-one years old. They each had two children. Although the bodies were not recovered, there were the pictures that Hayley, Cassie, and Linds had given to the police, which I guess was enough to identify the victims. Linds's Volvo was found burned and abandoned in northern New Jersey.

I immersed myself in online discussion boards where people tried to solve unsolved crimes. They called the four recent murders—the first in the Catskills, the second in the Helderbergs, and now these two in the Adirondacks—the Mountain Murders and talked about clues the police hadn't revealed to the public. I learned that in the first two murders the perpetrator cut off the last digit on the left pinky finger of the victims and likely kept them as trophies. No one—these awful know-it-alls on these discussion boards—knew whether the women Hayley found had missing digits. They were desperate to know and thought if they found out then these four murders could be linked to the same killer with certainty. I learned that the first two women had been poisoned, and the people on the discussion boards speculated the murderer could be a woman since women are more likely than men to use poison to kill. I spent so much time on those discussion boards, just lurking, never contributing, feeling animosity toward the people who posted. Everything about them irritated me, from their discussions about whether someone had to kill two people or three people to be called a serial killer, to how some labeled themselves "citizen detectives," to their speculations about why the killer dumped the bodies so close to what these online detectives only knew were "some campers."

When I got completely frustrated with reading the discussion boards, I soothed myself by watching competitive baking shows, because the worst thing that ever happened on one of those shows was a soufflé that wouldn't rise. I watched news reports about a virus that was spreading in Asia, but back then it felt so far away, something that could never touch me. I watched the Democratic presidential candidates' debate a few days before Christmas and thought about the Elizabeth Warren sticker Hayley had stuck on our dorm room door. I watched the debate on the television in my room with my AirPods in because I didn't want my parents to know that I wanted to learn about each of the Democratic candidates so I could cast my vote for one of them in November. I thought maybe if I became better informed about politics I would have more things to talk to Hayley about when we returned to campus.

I didn't hear from Hayley—or anyone else from school—over the break. I scrolled through Hayley's Instagram and saw she was having fun at home with her family and high school friends. Then

I saw that Linds and Cassie visited her in Rome for New Year's. I looked back at that email Hayley had sent me when we found out we were to be roommates and thought that if I could do it all over again, I would have responded more generously, would have tried to start a true conversation over email instead of writing only "Great, see you soon." And I wouldn't have waited six days to respond; I would have responded right away.

I was glad to see Hayley in our room when I arrived on campus after winter break. I noticed her two suitcases were under her bed, where she'd kept them throughout the fall before she'd moved into Cassie and Linds's room for the final week of the semester. Maybe she was back to stay.

She was at her desk with her laptop open and was typing something in a Word document when I'd entered the room. "Hey," she said, turning around to greet me, but not getting up from her chair.

"Hey," I said, rolling my suitcase into the room.

"Good break?" she said.

"Boring."

"Yeah," she said, nodding, but I knew from her Instagram that her break was far from boring, filled with fun activities with her family and friends from home and school.

"How are you?" I asked.

"Good, good," she said. "You?"

"Good," I said. And that was it. Hayley turned back to whatever she was typing, and I unpacked my suitcase and then shoved it under my bed. While I was down on my knees I saw that box of Diet Cokes, still unopened. I looked in our mini fridge and saw all those packaged pie slices from Thanksgiving. I gathered them up, took them down the hall, and dumped them into the large communal garbage can.

Six weeks of the spring semester went by uneventfully. Some nights Hayley stayed over with Cassie and Linds and some nights she stayed in our room. We never talked about what had happened on the Thanksgiving camping trip again. Around campus, I'd see Hayley with Cassie and Linds. The three of them were always together, as if they needed no one else. They ate all their meals together, and I always saw them studying at the same round table in the library. Every night the three of them went to the gym to run on treadmills. I thought of asking if I could join them, but I never ran on treadmills. Treadmills made me feel trapped; I preferred running through the neighborhoods surrounding campus.

Several frisbees appeared in our room. Hayley said Cassie and Linds were teaching her how to throw and catch. As soon as the season officially started after spring break, Hayley planned to join the ultimate team. She said the team focused on running and conditioning indoors until after spring break, when the fields would be dry enough to play on, and even though she wasn't on the team yet she was doing conditioning with Cassie and Linds. One night Cassie and Linds and the rest of the ultimate frisbee team had a dinner meeting at Bucca di Beppo. Since she was not officially on the team yet, Hayley was not invited to the meeting.

"You want to go to dinner?" she asked.

I looked up from my political science textbook. "Sure," I said. I tried to keep the excitement out of my voice.

It had been almost five months since I'd eaten a meal with Hayley. Often I ate by myself, or sometimes I ate with people who were in my classes, but I never particularly clicked with anyone. I was friendly enough but didn't pursue friendships beyond casual pleasantries.

We walked from our dorm to the dining hall at Sinclair Commons. As we made our way across campus, at least half a dozen people smiled and waved and said hello to Hayley. One girl with wavy hair that came halfway down her back ran up to us, giggling. She pulled a pink and yellow scrunchy off her wrist. "Oh my god, thank you for this," she said, holding the scrunchy out to Hayley.

Hayley laughed. "No problem."

"Oh, hey," the girl said to me. "I'm Jessa."

"Margaret," I said. I wondered how close Hayley and Jessa were; I wondered whether Jessa knew Hayley had stumbled onto murdered women during her Thanksgiving break. I wondered if I was the only one on this campus—besides Cassie and Linds—who knew this about Hayley.

"I showed up for my shift in the dining hall and realized I didn't have a hairband and I would get in trouble if I went in with my hair down, so Hayley took this scrunchy off her own head at the end of her shift and gave it to me and she literally saved my life," Jessa said.

"I guess she did," I said, even though what Jessa said was a melodramatic overstatement. I saw Hayley and Jessa shoot each other a look, as if I'd said something strange and unacceptable. Maybe the look had something to do with the fact that they both had to work in the dining hall and I did not. Maybe they thought I believed myself to be superior. Why was it always so hard with other people? Why had it been so easy with Hayley those first few weeks of the semester? Why didn't I feel strange and awkward talking to her back then? Could it have been that at first I thought I was cooler and more interesting than she was? Was it because I read her enthusiasm—that email right after we were assigned to be roommates, that quick Facebook friend request—as a sign that she was needy and friendless? Was it because initially I felt I had the upper hand that I'd been able to relax, to not be weird?

Jessa moved on, and Hayley and I went into the dining hall. "Are you still a vegetarian?" I asked.

"I'm a vegan now." We swiped our ID cards and got in the line for hot food.

"Oh," I said. "I didn't know. Is it hard being a vegan here?"

"Not really. There's always the salad bar and there's usually one vegan soup. And there's always a hot side that's vegan, and there's usually pasta, so I can put together a meal."

I felt self-conscious about my food choices. I wanted the buffalo chicken fingers, one of the few things the dining hall could prepare well, but I wasn't going to eat those in front of a vegan. I got a slice of pizza with no toppings and some sad-looking steamed broccoli, neither of which I really wanted.

We found a small table in the back of the dining hall, near one of the large windows. Hayley had constructed an enormous, colorful salad on her plate. "This is exactly where we sat the first time we had breakfast together!" she said.

"That's right." I couldn't believe she remembered. We'd dined at this table the first day of classes in the fall. We'd both been excited that we could serve ourselves unlimited amounts of bacon and each piled a plate high with it.

"Sometimes I think back to the beginning of the year and wish it could be like that again," Hayley said.

"You do?" I said, surprised.

"It was nice back then. Everything seemed, I don't know, easy."

"Yeah. I miss those days too. I miss you."

Hayley looked at me for a long moment without saying anything, and then suddenly I felt embarrassed and my face warmed. I had been talking about our friendship. She had been talking about the days before she'd found two murdered women.

"You should join some clubs," Hayley finally said.

"Like what?"

"I don't know. What do you like to do? You know your tuition money isn't just paying for classes. It pays for clubs and stuff too. That's why I try to do so much stuff on campus. It's like going to a buffet and getting your money's worth, you know? Just going to classes is like eating Jell-O and skipping everything else at the buffet."

My family did not go to buffets. No one in my family ever spoke about getting their money's worth. In fact, money was almost never spoken of, except when my sister was being chastised about wasting money by wanting to pursue an English major.

"Are you still part of the Outdoors Club?" I asked. This was the closest I'd come to talking to Hayley about what had happened during Thanksgiving break.

She shook her head but didn't seem upset. "I figure I'll get outdoors enough with ultimate. Hey!" she said, brightening. "*You* should try out for ultimate!"

"Me?" I said. Why would she want me to be part of the world she was building with Cassie and Linds?

"Yeah, you," Hayley said. "You run every day. Running is a big part of the game. I've been trying to build up my stamina, but you go for these long runs, so you'd be great."

"You'd want me to join the team?" I asked. Ultimate seemed like something that did not belong to me, something that was the property of Hayley, Cassie, Linds, and other health-exuding smiling girls with high ponytails. I was someone with pale skin and thick glasses and hair that frizzed around my face, even when I tried to pull it back; I would never look like I belonged with them.

"It would be fun," Hayley said. "We could spend time together again." I wasn't sure if she was just trying to be kind, if she was trying to get me to feel less embarrassed about saying I missed her. But then she smiled and it seemed genuine, and it seemed we could be friends again.

"And it would help me get a good value out of my college education," I said. I'd meant it as a joke, but I was unsure if I'd come across as elitist or snarky, but then Hayley laughed and said, "Yes, *totally*," and I felt buoyed, felt like our ship was finally righting.

I wish I could say I joined the ultimate frisbee team and became not only close friends with Hayley, Cassie, and Linds but also with everyone else on the team. I wish I could say I ate dinner every night with the team. I wish I could say I learned to balance fun extracurriculars with academics. I wish I could say I grew tan from the afternoons in the sunshine playing ultimate, and I realized a high ponytail was the best way to keep my hair out of my face as I ran across a field and caught the frisbees Hayley threw to me. I wish I could say I had so much fun with my new ultimate friends that I decided to live with them in an on-campus apartment during the summer.

But of course none of that happened. By the beginning of March that virus I thought was confined to Asia was spreading across Europe and beginning to crop up in the United States. I was worried about it in a mild way, like how everyone is worried about getting cancer—it's a possibility, but it's not something anyone ever believes will happen to them until it does. I thought we would be fine. I thought my freshman year would have bookends, a handful of weeks at the beginning and end of the year when I was happy and had people to eat meals with and to spend time with. But of course none of that happened.

What happened was that the night before spring break started, Hayley put on her robe and I thought she went to take a shower. She forgot to take her phone with her; usually, she slipped it into the pocket of her robe when she went to shower. This was the first time since Thanksgiving that Hayley had left her phone unattended. I picked up her phone and punched in her passcode, which I knew was her birthday: 0904 for September 4th. I'd seen her punch it in so many times, and I suppose I should have averted my eyes, but I thought maybe one day, in some sort of emergency situation, I might need to have access to her contacts.

Of course what I wanted to see were the photos Hayley had taken of the women she, Cassie, and Linds found. There had been no breaks in the case and no more murders in the mountains upstate. No one seemed interested in the case anymore; the posts on the discussion boards I read during winter break had petered out. But what might happen if I could find and post a photo of the women? Maybe that would make people excited again to figure out what had happened, maybe the case could be solved, and maybe that would bring some sort of comfort to Hayley. I found the photo gallery on Hayley's phone and scrolled down to the pictures from the end of November. I found several blurry, dimly lit photos of Hayley, Cassie, and Linds, Hayley's arm outstretched to take the selfies, the other hand holding up a charred marshmallow on a stick. I found another photo of Hayley inside the tent with her SleepPhones and eye mask on, her arms held out like a zombie as she sat up in her sleeping bag. There were no photos of the dead women, and I assumed Hayley had deleted them after sending them to the police. But then I had an idea. I looked at the albums in her gallery and saw one titled 11.30. The first photo in that album—the one that showed in the thumbnail for the album—was just a photo of the outside of their tent. But November 30th was the day they'd found the bodies. I clicked on the album. And there they were. Five photos of the bodies. I wanted to AirDrop them to my phone, but before I did I opened one and was about to zoom in on the left hand to see if I could see a missing digit on the pinky, but then Hayley came back into the room, holding a can of Diet Coke, her hair not wet from the shower.

"What are you doing?" she asked.

I tried to close the album, but she'd already seen what I was looking at.

"What's wrong with you?" she asked.

"Why are you back so soon?"

"I just brought a soda back from the refrigerator down the hall. I was going to drop it off and then shower."

"We have a refrigerator," I said. I was still holding Hayley's phone, and she grabbed it from me.

"If you haven't noticed, our refrigerator smells," said Hayley, slamming her Diet Coke onto her desk. She slipped her phone into the pocket of her robe. "You know my passcode?"

"I just tried your birthday."

"How do you know my birthday?"

"Facebook," I said. Her birthday was a few days before school began. Back in early September I was still feeling superior, so I didn't wish my soon-to-be roommate a happy birthday. I just sat back and watched as dozens and dozens of people posted their good wishes.

"Why would you want to see those pictures?"

"Why do you still have them?" I said, hoping to deflect the question.

"I don't think you're in any position to be asking questions," Hayley said as she turned and left to go to the showers down the hall. As she walked away, I could see the outline of her phone in her robe pocket.

There was no time to fix what I'd done. After her shower, Hayley packed her two suitcases and her backpack and said she would spend the night with Cassie and Linds and then she'd see about things after spring break. There would only be seven weeks left of the semester after we got back, she said, and maybe she'd spend them all with Cassie and Linds. I thought it best not to plead with her at that point. I thought we would have time after break, that the break would allow me to come up with an apology that was sufficient. So I just watched her go, said nothing as she rolled her suitcases out of our shared room.

And of course what happened was that we all went home and then we stayed home. The virus turned out to be more virulent than most Americans expected at first, and in the middle of our spring break we were told the rest of the semester would be conducted online. We would not return to campus.

I wished I was as old as my sister, who was living on her own in Philadelphia, where she was attending medical school. I wished I had somewhere to go that wasn't my parents' house. My father, who spent much of my life traveling for business, was now home all the time. He spent most of his waking hours either on conference calls with his colleagues or staring at the television. My mother spent the mornings puttering around the house or garden, as though she had always been the one to clean the house or tend the garden, instead of the hired help. She spent afternoons looking at restaurant websites and figuring out what takeout to order for dinner.

I went for a long run every morning. One day my mother suggested that she come with me, but I had never seen her run and worried she would slow me down. She kept slim by doing Pilates, but the studio where she took classes had closed. She refused to keep up with the classes via Zoom because she thought there was something unsettling about looking at a screen and seeing everyone's homes. "I just thought running might be a nice activity for us to do together," my mother said.

"I run so I can be alone," I told her, and she told me one day I'd regret always wanting to be alone.

After my daily run and a breakfast of oatmeal and half a grapefruit, I spent my days in my bedroom, staring at my computer. First I worked on my online classes. I usually finished my work in just a few hours. I wanted to ask for more work to keep me busy, but it didn't seem like the right time to bother my professors. I checked social media to see what people were up to, and it seemed most people I knew were baking complicated and time-consuming bread or learning to sew masks. I knew how to do neither of those things, nor did I particularly want to learn. I looked to see if there was any progress on finding the person who'd killed the women. The case seemed to have gone cold. I waited to see if anyone from school would text or email, but no one did, except for my professors, who kept sending emails to the students in their classes explaining how they were changing the syllabi. I sent Hayley a text telling her I hoped she was staying healthy. I didn't apologize for looking at the photos on her phone. I thought I'd save that for when I could see her in person again. Hayley didn't respond.

I downloaded all sorts of self-improvement apps. They kept me reasonably distracted. Each day I practiced planks and sit-ups, guided by a cartoon figure on my phone. I had another app that suggested small daily changes to improve my sleep hygiene. I decided I would learn several languages while I was forced to stay at home. I downloaded programs to teach me Japanese, Russian, Swahili, and Italian. I decided to start with Italian. I didn't get far because I kept pressing PLAY on the screen with the word *ciao* on it, which then played a woman's voice saying the word. I imagined it would be the first word I said when I saw Hayley again, but *ciao* as in hello, not good-bye. I pressed the PLAY button on the app, pressed it again and again, so *ciao, ciao, ciao, ciao* repeated, an endless loop in my otherwise silent room.

PERSPECTIVE FOR ARTISTS

We were the art girls. We had charcoal under our fingernails, flecks of dried clay on our jeans, acrylic paint in our hair. The artsy seniors always lived on the second floor of McAllister Hall; it was tradition. Although our boarding school, Florence Summer Academy for Girls, was beautiful—the dorms looked like magnificent stone castles—the inside of McAllister Hall was so run down that whoever lived on the second floor was allowed to paint the walls of their rooms. Each fall, Facilities delivered cans of primer so last year's walls could be painted over and new masterpieces created.

The fall of our senior year, we picked up paint rollers and shouted, "This is for Mrs. Lawrence!" Mrs. Lawrence was our art teacher, who'd retired in May. She'd purchased an RV and was traveling the country with her husband and cat and had promised to send postcards from every state and tourist attraction they visited. When we arrived back at school on the first of September, we sprinted into the front office and asked Ruth, the secretary, if any postcards were waiting for us. She shook her head and said, "I'm sure they're on the way."

Had Mrs. Lawrence forgotten about us? We needed her to remember us. We were seniors, we would be applying to art schools, and where would we be without Mrs. Lawrence's letters of recommendation? She thought we were brilliant, geniuses; she called us her little Mary Cassatts, her baby Georgia O'Keeffes, miniature Frida Kahlos. There were other nicknames, too: My Lovelies, My Bumblebees, My Buttercups. During the three years she was our teacher, it never occurred to us that perhaps she hadn't bothered to actually learn our names. It hadn't mattered then. She was so complimentary, so certain of our talent and our bright futures, that all we could do was love her.

How would we track down Mrs. Lawrence if we had no idea where in the country she was? This was before email, before Facebook; this was a time when someone could disappear if they wanted to. But it was September, the campus was bursting forth in green, the dorms airy and sun-filled and smelling of lemon wood polish. We could not stay worried for long.

And there was good news, too. There was a new art teacher, and the principal told us she was young and very talented and had just moved upstate from Manhattan. When we walked into the art classroom, our hearts leapt. The new teacher looked like an artist. Mrs. Lawrence had worn oversized floral caftans, black stretchy pants, orthopedic shoes. She was shaped like an eggplant and had a slow, lumbering walk. She wore two or three bulky necklaces all at once and rings on every finger and perfume that filled the room with the scent of lilacs. Although she was always dressed in bursts of bright colors, Mrs. Lawrence didn't seem like an artist to us. She talked about unartistic things, like making meatloaf for her husband for dinner or how she kept forgetting to trim her cat's claws. But this new teacher was tall and thin and wore only black. Her short hair was dyed an almost white blonde and her lipstick was crimson. She was from New York City. Some of us came from Manhattan and proclaimed the new teacher looked like the students who smoked cigarettes outside of the School of Visual Arts. Mrs. Lawrence was someone who taught art; this new teacher looked like someone who *did* art.

Before she even spoke, we liked her. We thought that in just one semester we could impress her enough that she could write us stunning letters of recommendation for RISD and Pratt and Parsons. We loved young teachers, but they were a rarity at Florence Summer the years we attended. Our physical education teacher, Mr. Baker, was young, and when it snowed he'd gather trays from the cafeteria and go sledding with us and somehow convince the cooks to have Swiss Miss in Styrofoam cups waiting for us when we came back inside to return the icy trays. We hoped for more of this sort of fun with the new art teacher. Maybe she'd take us to Paris to see the great museums and sneak us into nightclubs, insisting we were old enough to be admitted.

We wondered how old the new art teacher was. If she was right out of college then she'd only be four or five years older than us. Maybe she could be our friend. Maybe she could be our confidant, someone we'd go to with our questions about roommates and boys and college choices.

Once we were seated, the new teacher smiled at us, a tentative smile, and said, "Welcome to Senior Art Intensive. I'm Miss Holloway. I'm new." Her voice was quiet, and she seemed almost scared of us, as if we might suddenly stand up and fling paintbrushes at her head. Her coolness instantly dissolved. "Maybe we could go around and you can each tell me your name?" She said this as if she was unsure whether we'd comply. We told her our names and she checked each name off a roster. "I'll do my best to learn your names quickly," she said when we were done. She bent and picked up a stack of books from a shelf. "This will be your first textbook for the semester. Please pass them around." The book was called *Perspective for Artists* and had a pencil sketch of a cityscape on the cover.

We gaped at each other. *Textbook? First* textbook? There would be more books? We'd never had textbooks for art. We were just creative, made things, did whatever we wanted. And, always, all of us got As. For all of the previous year, Mrs. Lawrence had rolled a TV on a black cart into the classroom, and we'd watched *Days of Our Lives* while we drew and painted and sculpted. Mrs. Lawrence said true artists needed to understand torture and anguish, and soap operas would teach us all of these things. How could we go from *Days of Our Lives* to *Perspective for Artists*?

"Let's start with some definitions," Miss Holloway said. She walked to the blackboard in the corner of the classroom that Mrs. Lawrence had never used. She wrote "vanishing point," "multiple-point perspective," "single-point perspective," "rule of thirds," and "parallel lines." She smiled at us and said, "I'm sure you all know about parallel lines from math class." We didn't smile back. How dare she invoke math class in a room that was supposed to be free of rules, free of terms scrawled on chalkboards, free of textbooks?

We looked at each other and shook our heads. We longed for the days when Mrs. Lawrence would heave a large rectangle of clay onto the center of the table and say, "Have at it, my little sparrows." Miss Holloway explained the terms on the board and told us our first graded assignment, due on Friday, was to draw one of the buildings on campus. She told us we shouldn't turn in our first try; we should keep drawing until we had something we were happy with, even if it took fifty or a hundred tries. "One hundred tries?" mouthed Dana Jordan.

Miss Holloway drew a three-dimensional cube on the board and told us we had to first master drawing cubes and then cylinders before we should try drawing buildings, and it might be a good idea to spend the next day or two drawing only shapes. She handed us each a 2B graphite stick and a pad of newsprint. We looked at each other again. We weren't even allowed to choose our own materials?

"Why are we going to be graded on this?" Tia Murphy said.

"Aren't assignments always graded?" Miss Holloway asked. Her brow wrinkled.

"Mrs. Lawrence did something she called holistic grading," said Bella Weatherwax.

"What does that mean?" said Miss Holloway.

"It means she didn't give us any grades during the semester and then at the end of the semester she'd think back and evaluate each of us on all the work we did over the semester," Bella said.

"I think it would be easier for me to keep track of things if I grade each assignment along the way," Miss Holloway said.

Amanda Chung raised her hand.

"Yes, Amanda?" Miss Holloway said. How had she learned her name so quickly? She hadn't even looked down at her roster.

"But how do you grade *art*?" Amanda said. "Shouldn't we get As if we try and if we're creative?"

"You don't *get* As. You *earn* As," Miss Holloway said. "Just the same as in every other class."

We didn't like that answer. Maybe in other courses you earned As if you could graph a function or recite facts about the War of 1812 or explain the symbolism of the green light in *The Great Gatsby*. You could earn As in classes where there were right answers and wrong answers, but in art, we were certain, there were no wrong answers.

Throughout the fall we stopped into the front office, and again and again Ruth told us no postcards had arrived. "I'll let you know, girls, I promise, if one does come," she said.

"Do you maybe know where Mrs. Lawrence is?" asked Sandra Rios. It was what we all wanted to know, but we didn't want to hear that Mrs. Lawrence was keeping in touch with the adults but had decided to abandon us.

Ruth put her right hand over her heart and said, "I swear, I have no idea where that woman went off to. And let me tell you, I'd like to know because she took off with my Crock-Pot." Then Ruth's face turned pink, and she added, "I've said enough."

Mrs. Lawrence's silence wasn't the only thing that troubled us that fall; throughout the first semester, someone kept vandalizing our campus. Students parked cars in a lot on the east side of campus, and one morning we woke to find that every car parked there had a deep silver scratch on its side. In late October, someone painted DIE RICH BITCHES on the front entrance of McAllister Hall in dripping orange paint. We suspected it was done by people from town, probably kids who went to the public school who thought we were elitists and that Florence Summer Academy for Girls was nothing more than a finishing school for millionaires' daughters. But this wasn't true. Many of us were on scholarship. A lot of our fathers worked in upstate pulp and paper mills and sawmills. Many of our parents were state workers stuck in cubicles in Albany, making enough to land our families in the middle class but not earning enough to afford tuition at Florence Summer. Over half the student body was on work-study, serving meals in the dining hall, shelving books in the library, planting flowers outside the academic buildings in the spring. Yes, there were parents who were executives with KeyBank or Fleet Bank or who had enormous offices on high floors in buildings on Wall Street; their daughters got red Jeeps for their seventeenth birthdays, spent summers in Europe. But that wasn't everyone.

By November, we dreaded leaving our dorms in the mornings, afraid to see what sort of destruction we'd see. The morning before Thanksgiving break, the stained glass windows of the Great Hall had been smashed; someone had managed this despite the extra security that now patrolled campus as though it were a prison. It was our last year at Florence Summer; it was supposed to be our best year, but nothing was going as we'd anticipated.

Matters did not improve with Miss Holloway as the semester progressed. She continued with her lessons and the books, moving from perspective to composition to color. She would spend ten or fifteen minutes showing us how to properly use a stick of charcoal or a T-square. She gave lectures about different types and weights of paper. She made us draw our nondominant hand fifty times and turn in all fifty sketches before we were allowed to move on to the next assignment. Art had gone from our favorite class to our most despised. Mrs. Lawrence had let us switch mediums or even switch projects whenever we got bored. Now our only outlet, our only escape, were the walls of our dorm rooms, which we splattered with fluorescent paint, drew zigzags across, drew crooked lines on without using rulers. Then we mocked Miss Holloway by saying, "An artist must first learn two things. How to draw a precise circle and how to draw a straight line. And there are tools that can help you do that." We'd cackle and draw lopsided circles until our walls looked like they were being taken over by enormous amoebas.

We spent much of the fall semester being nervous about our letters of recommendation. We still could not track down Mrs. Lawrence and time was running out for our art school applications. The more charitable among us decided that Mrs. Lawrence's husband had driven the RV into the Grand Canyon and they were both dead and this was the only reason Mrs. Lawrence was not staying in touch. But the pragmatists had begun to realize that perhaps she'd never loved us as much as we had loved her. The job had been a paycheck, and she'd just been putting in time until she could retire. Perhaps our love had been false. Maybe we didn't love her; maybe we'd only loved hearing how wonderful and talented we were, and now Miss Holloway made us wonder whether anything Mrs. Lawrence had said was true at all.

Right before winter break, the seniors went on a field trip to the roller rink. There, we were allowed to eat popcorn and hot dogs, drink soda until we were jittery with caffeine and sugar, and stuff quarters into the coin-operated vending machines to buy gum, candy, and small plastic trinkets. Our chaperones were Miss Holloway and our gym teacher, Mr. Baker. Mr. Baker immediately put on a pair of rented brown skates and skated with us under the pulsing red and blue and green lights of the rink. He was good; he could even skate backward. When "Ice Ice Baby" came on over the loudspeakers, Mr. Baker rapped along, and we had to hold our stomachs because we were laughing so hard. Miss Holloway stood by the snack stand and sipped a can of Sprite through a straw and watched us circle the rink. "Robots are fueled by Sprite?" Sabrina Fox said, and we all giggled. We'd started calling Miss Holloway The Robot behind her back. We thought she had no life outside of teaching art and that she lived only to force us to complete one tiresome exercise after another.

After about half an hour of skating, Mr. Baker rolled to the edge of the rink and shouted, "You ever going to join me?" We waited for Miss Holloway's answer and wished the music would quiet down the way it would during an important scene in a movie. All year we'd wondered about Miss Holloway's personal life, wondered who she went home to at night. *If* she went home to anyone. We were convinced she went home and drew her hands and three-dimensional cubes all night until her eyes could no longer stay open. And here was Mr. Baker, who maybe wasn't the smartest guy and wore blue polo shirts and khaki pants and gray New Balance sneakers every single day, but he was one of the few men on our campus and he was funny and knew all the words to "Ice Ice Baby" and let us go sledding on cafeteria trays. Could Miss Holloway do any better? We didn't think so. But Miss Holloway smiled and said, "I'll just watch, thank you." We looked at each other, shook our heads. And then Eliza Hofstadter whispered, "Maybe The Robot needs new batteries." We laughed again, high on the freedom of a night out and too much sugar. What we didn't consider then was that maybe Miss Holloway didn't skate because she knew that if she did, we'd find something to critique; one way or another, we'd find something to mock.

We returned from winter break well-fed, well-rested, and with new haircuts and new sweaters. That year the style was oversized wool cardigans, the kind our grandfathers wore. We were ready to face another frozen, gray upstate winter, ready to hunker down for a few months and study until we got into college and could finally relax. We hadn't gotten our letters of recommendation from Mrs. Lawrence. Instead we'd gotten letters from our English teachers, our history teachers, even our science teachers. We asked, as politely as we could, if they might include something about our artwork in their letters, in light of Mrs. Lawrence's disappearance. We hoped a few kind words about us as artists, along with the portfolios we'd assembled, might be enough, but we were nervous that we wouldn't get into art schools. We were afraid to ask Miss Holloway for recommendations. She'd given us bad grades when we'd done sloppy work on our assignments; we no longer had all As in art.

Over break there had been more damage on campus: a small fire set in the auditorium that had burned a hole in the wooden stage, obscene words spray painted on the dorms, and, on the day we returned to school, six Japanese Cherry trees that had been brought to the academy twenty-five years before by a Japanese ambassador whose daughter attended the school were hacked down. Whoever was doing this was sneaky and quick. They still hadn't been caught. The people who were damaging our beautiful, calm school knew nothing of us. They thought we were terrible people, and we hated being hated.

We returned, grumpy, to the art classroom in January. Our final semester of school was supposed to be fun, but Senior Art Intensive lasted all year so none of us could wiggle out of it. Miss Holloway wore more clothing than she had during the fall semester, including a thin, filmy black scarf that wrapped around and around her neck, as if she needed an extra layer of protection from us. She looked tired and had gray circles under her eyes, but she smiled at us, greeted each of us by name, asked how our breaks had been. "Fine," we said. No one wanted to divulge any more details to her. "I'd like to give you girls a choice about the work you'll do this semester," she said. We sat up straighter. "As you know, the spring drama is *Little Women*," she said. Oh, we knew. Students had begun to whisper about it in the fall, and we knew who'd star in the play: Missy Filbert, Anna Cavanaugh, Laurel Propetti, and Kimberly Allendale. Mrs. Horace, the drama teacher, played favorites. It was always the same girls who got the leads in every school production.

Some of us had been tempted to audition, wanting to be Jo, the tomboy, or Beth—how romantic to die young! Of course the most natural fit would have been Amy, the artist. But you couldn't just start being one of the drama kids the last semester of senior year. If any of us had talent for acting it would have been discovered already. "I spoke with Mrs. Horace last week, and she invited us to make sets for the play." Miss Holloway grinned, and we could see how excited she was to be offering us this opportunity.

We were silent for a few seconds, then Dawn Karimi said, "You said you'd give us a choice. What's the other option?"

"The other option would be to go on as we did last semester, learning new techniques, learning how to use new materials. But I think we covered so much last semester that you would be able to help create beautiful sets."

It was clear what Miss Holloway wanted us to choose. It sounded as if she'd already committed us to Mrs. Horace.

"Take a minute. Talk it over. Decide," said Miss Holloway, but her eyes darted fast between us, as if she already knew what our answer would be.

We leaned our heads together and whispered. We didn't have to talk for long. "We'll continue with our lessons," said Tamara Silver.

"Are you sure?" said Miss Holloway. She grabbed onto the edge of a wooden drafting table and held onto it hard, as if she were dizzy. "This is your final decision?"

"This is our final decision," said Tamara.

And so we continued with our lessons, slowly, despite ourselves, learning about color and composition and perspective and light. We absorbed terms like verisimilitude, analogous colors, and reflected light because Miss Holloway said them so often. Although we studied art vocabulary and learned how to use artists' tools and better understood how to look at the paintings Miss Holloway projected onto a screen at the front of the classroom, we went about our lessons halfheartedly. We knew we needed to pass this class if we wanted to go to college—and every graduate of Florence Summer was expected to go to college—so we did what Miss Holloway asked of us, but mostly we didn't do a good job on our assignments. We just wanted to pass.

At least we could be as creative as we wanted with our dorm room walls. In February Bella Weatherwax called Facilities and asked if they'd deliver more primer. We were tired of our zigzagged lines, our free-form amoebic blobs. We painted everything white and started again. But this time something strange happened. What appeared on the walls of each of our rooms was better than anything we could have done in the past. Dawn Karimi painted a field of sunflowers that looked like they were waving in the wind. Sandra Rios painted a cityscape of her hometown of Jersey City, the view from her bedroom window in her family's apartment. "Now when I get homesick I just look at my wall," she said. Tamara Silver painted animals from Australia—a koala, an emu, a wallaby—life-sized on her wall. She'd gone to the Australian Outback over the summer and couldn't wait to go back.

While we were busy with our walls, Miss Holloway worked alone on the sets for *Little Women*. After school and during her free periods we'd see Miss Holloway hauling lumber from a pickup truck to the art classroom. We heard her hammering together frames for the sets late into the night. We watched as the canvases she stretched across the lumber filled with color. We were impressed with Miss Holloway's work. We'd never seen Mrs. Lawrence draw or paint anything, but the sets proved Miss Holloway knew what she was talking about. She painted a set for Beth's room and one for a garden and one for the March family living room. One day Mrs. Horace, the drama teacher, came into the classroom during Senior Art Intensive and looked at Miss Holloway's work, which leaned against the back wall. "My god, Kelly," she said, "why aren't you on Broadway working on sets there?" She stared at the sets for a long while then turned to us. We were working on graded watercolor washes, each of us selecting one color and working from dark to light down a page. "Girls, you must feel so lucky to have Miss Holloway as your teacher," she said.

We smiled at her, nodded, but no one said anything. What was there to say?

By the end of March the sets had been finished and were moved to the auditorium. By then, some of us had gotten into art schools and others had been rejected. Some of us were on waitlists, and it was a tense, eager time. The actors practiced late every night, and we were all excited to see the show when it opened the second week of April. The spring drama was a big deal; it marked the beginning of Parents' Weekend, and the auditorium was always packed.

On the first Friday in April, as we walked toward the dining hall for breakfast, we heard wails coming from the auditorium. We were filled with both curiosity and fear, and we ran over to the auditorium, pushed the doors open, and sprinted inside. Someone had destroyed Miss Holloway's sets in the middle of the night. The wood had been sawed through, and the canvases had been splattered with black paint then sliced until the canvas hung in strips. We watched in silence as Miss Holloway surveyed the damage, weeping. She touched the canvases, and her fingers came away stained with still-wet paint. "Why?" she said. Then "Who?" She looked at us, and we were horrified. We understood she thought we had something to do with this.

Mr. Baker ran into the auditorium and took the steps two at a time. He ran to Miss Holloway and folded her in his arms. "It's okay, Kelly," he said. "It's okay."

"The play's in a week," she said. She allowed him to hold her while we watched, and we wondered if there was something more to their relationship that we hadn't been privy to.

"Here's an idea," said Mr. Baker, releasing Miss Holloway. "What if you girls help Miss Holloway redo the sets?"

"Oh, no," said Miss Holloway, shaking her head. "They don't want to do that."

Mr. Baker looked at us and waited for one of us to say something, but no one did. So he said, "Tell her, girls. Tell her you'll help."

Mr. Baker seemed different. We'd never seen him be anything but jovial and cheerful, the goof, the campus jester. But now there was something pleading in his voice and in his eyes, and he seemed to indicate that only we could right what had gone wrong. Miss Holloway stood next to him, her scarf wrapped tightly around her thin neck, and continued to shake her head.

"Why would they fix something they destroyed?" Miss Holloway said. "They hate me. They call me The Robot. I've heard them whispering."

We were shocked that Miss Holloway knew our nickname for her. We wondered what else she knew. Mr. Baker looked at the destroyed sets and then at us. "No," he said. "These girls couldn't have done this."

"It doesn't matter if they did or they didn't," Miss Holloway said. "I don't want their help."

And then she ran from the auditorium and left us standing with Mr. Baker next to the ruined sets and no one knew what to say. Finally, Mr. Baker looked at us and said, "Well, go on to breakfast. There's nothing more that can be done here."

Miss Holloway was late for Senior Art Intensive that day. We wondered if she would even show up, but we waited silently. When she finally came in, she was pushing the TV on the rolling cart in front of her. She handed Sabrina Fox the remote and said, "Go ahead. Put on whatever you want."

"Do we have an assignment?" Sabrina said.

"Do whatever you want," said Miss Holloway. Her voice was quiet, dull. "It's what you wanted all year, isn't it?"

It had been what we'd longed for, but now that the television was back in the room, no one wanted to watch it. We felt adrift. We wanted a lesson. We wanted so much: we wanted to be able to tell Miss Holloway about our dorm room walls, about how those lessons helped us paint scenes we would have never been able to create before. We wanted to tell her how sorry we were, and we wanted to make sure she knew we hadn't destroyed her sets.

"How did you know about the TV?" said Tamara.

Miss Holloway laughed, a dry, brittle sound. "You really want to know? In the teachers' lounge everyone makes fun of your old teacher. They say she checked out a decade ago, that she resorted to letting you all watch TV during class every day. They said something about soap operas. Everyone was waiting for her to retire so they could hire someone to actually teach art. But you girls are ruined. You don't want to learn. You just want free rein, and that's what you'll get for the rest of the year."

"We don't," said Amanda. "We want lessons."

"It's too late to want that," said Miss Holloway. "Just too late."

Mrs. Horace rented sets for *Little Women*. They were adequate, but we could not help but picture what Miss Holloway's sets would have looked like in place of the rented ones. The show was a success, and our parents cheered and clapped, but we sat in the audience feeling guilty with no way to remedy what had gone wrong.

A week before the end of the school year Ruth, the front office secretary, entered the art classroom waving a postcard in the air. Miss Holloway looked up from the book on Renaissance paintings she was reading. Now she read art books each day in class, and we were free to do whatever we chose. We'd taken to doing exercises out of the textbooks she'd passed out to us throughout the year. At the end of each class period we brought our sketches and exercises up to Miss Holloway's table and left them for her. The next day, they were where we'd left them, untouched. We collected our work and began new exercises. We hoped we could say with pencils and paints what we couldn't say with words, but Miss Holloway didn't want to hear anything from us. Each day she rolled the TV cart into the classroom and handed one of us the remote. We never turned on the TV, just quietly set the remote down and worked in uncomfortable silence.

"I'm so sorry to interrupt class," Ruth said. "It's just that all year the girls have been asking about Mrs. Lawrence, and wouldn't you know it, right before they graduate here's a postcard from her!" Ruth handed the postcard to Miss Holloway. "I couldn't wait to give it to them. I just finished sorting the mail."

"Thank you, Ruth," Miss Holloway said. "How nice of you."

Ruth turned to us and said, "I knew you'd all be so excited."

Miss Holloway held the card up. "Who wants it?" she asked.

No one answered.

"Now don't everyone jump up at once," Ruth said. She laughed, but no one laughed along with her. She looked perplexed. "How about you read it out loud, Kelly?"

"Okay," said Miss Holloway. She flipped the postcard over and read: "My Sweet Petunias, Sorry to not have written sooner, but I'm sure you're all doing swimmingly. I'm certain hundreds of masterpieces were created this year! I am in Florida now, and we may settle here permanently. What beautiful water and blue, blue skies. And no New York winters. Imagine that! Congratulations, girls, on graduation. You all have such bright futures ahead of you. xoxo, Mrs. Lawrence."

"Well, isn't that nice," said Ruth.

"Yes, nice," said Miss Holloway, flipping the postcard over and studying the palm trees on the front.

But it wasn't nice; it was generic and unspecific, and it had come too late to mean anything. Mrs. Lawrence had hidden from us all year. She hadn't helped us at all. Those of us who got into art school believed we got in *despite* Mrs. Lawrence. And, maybe, those of us who'd been accepted had gotten in because of what we'd learned from Miss Holloway.

Ruth waited with an expectant look on her face.

"Thank you, Ruth," said Dawn, and then we all echoed her thanks. We wanted to say nothing about the content of the postcard, so instead we heaped thanks on Ruth, which satisfied her enough that she left the room. Once Ruth was gone, Miss Holloway put the postcard on our table, but no one reached for it, and finally, three days later it finally disappeared. The janitor likely swept it into the garbage with the other scraps of paper we left on the table.

On the last day of school, Dana Jordan called Facilities and asked if they would bring one more batch of primer to us. Two men came that afternoon and placed silver cans of primer outside our doors for the third time that year. We painted our walls again, adding layer over layer until everything was thoroughly covered and we could not see what was below. We left our walls white and plain when we moved out, and we hoped the girls who lived on the second floor of McAllister Hall the next year would paint over them, would do better than we had done.

SINCE VINCENT LEFT

After my marriage dissolved, I was left with the dogs, which Vincent, my ex, said was fair since I was the one who'd wanted them in the first place. He said I'd wanted the dogs the way a child wants pets: first exuberant and enthusiastic, then my interest quickly waning when I realized that much of dog ownership consists of scooping shit, hauling home fifty-pound bags of dog food, and constantly using a lint roller on my wardrobe of mostly black clothing. Vincent said it was my fault I was stuck with two dogs instead of one because I had insisted that if we brought home only one dog it would get lonely while we both were at work.

On the day the divorce became official, I was at the dog park a few blocks from the home Vincent and I used to share, which I now shared with only the dogs. I had argued that I should keep the home if I was keeping the dogs since it was ideally situated near the dog park. During our negotiations Vincent and I had been seated across a wooden table, he with his lawyer to his right, me with my lawyer on my left. Vincent's broken right arm was in a sling; it had been seven months since he'd broken it, and instead of healing smoothly he'd had to have two surgeries, and he blamed me for this. "Fine, Amy, fine, take the house," Vincent had said, waving his good hand dismissively as if I were a haggler at a garage sale, trying to talk him down from fifty cents to a dime for an old record.

At the dog park that day, I kept thinking of the word divorcée, which was what I officially was. Divorcée, divorcée, I repeated in my mind as Gunner and Rufus ran after the slobber-covered tennis ball I tossed.

"Beautiful dogs," said a man wearing rolled-up dark jeans, a red-and-black checked flannel shirt, and suspenders. He cradled a Pomeranian in the crook of his left arm. The dog's tongue hung out of the side of its mouth and its eyes were slightly crossed, and I wondered whether these issues were the result of overbreeding. It did not look like the man had any intention of putting the dog on the ground, so I wanted to know why he'd even brought it to the dog park. The man had a mustache with curled up ends as though he were a strongman in a 1920s circus. He was my age, late thirties, too old for the hipster urban lumberjack getup. "What breeds are they?" he asked, gesturing toward my dogs with the hand that was not full of Pomeranian. Gunner had given up on chasing the tennis ball and had collapsed in a panting heap of gray fur in the shade of a tree. Rufus was attacking the tennis ball vigorously, growling as he gnawed on it.

They were mutts. Pound dogs. Adopted-before-they-could-be-gassed dogs. "That one," I said, pointing at Gunner, "he's a snuffle retriever. And the little one, he's a blue marmoset schnauzer." I waited for the lumberjack to tell me I was ridiculous.

"Right, right," he said. "I thought so."

"Rare breeds," I said. "Expensive."

"Of course," said the man. He brought a finger to his face and caressed his mustache. "Rare and expensive," he echoed.

I read once in a women's magazine that life has three prongs: your personal life, your work life, and your home life. Home life refers only to your actual abode, not what goes on inside of it.

The magazine said you could only realistically expect to be happy with two prongs of your life at any one point. I wanted to say that at this juncture I was only happy with my home life, but happy wasn't exactly the word. I possessed a home, but I wasn't particularly happy in it, mostly because it had fallen into a state of disrepair since Vincent left.

After I got home from talking to the lumberjack at the dog park, I bent to wipe Gunner's and Rufus's muddy feet with paper towels and realized how overwhelmingly my house smelled of wet dog and how everything—including the white carpet—was covered in muddy footprints. I suppose I should admit that some of the footprints were mine. Vincent had been the one to clean, had always reminded me to take off my shoes by the door, had somehow kept the carpets the color of fresh snow, had gotten the dirt and footprints off the kitchen tile, had kept the whole place from smelling like drowned dogs.

The phone rang, and caller ID displayed an unfamiliar local number. Rufus howled, as he always did when the phone rang. I thought I must have forgotten another appointment, maybe with the dentist, maybe at the car dealership to get my snow tires on, maybe at the groomer to get Gunner's and Rufus's fur trimmed. When I picked up the phone, I was disappointed to learn it was Dale Grommet, the chair of the English Department.

"Amy?" he said. He sounded tired, troubled.

"Is everything okay?" I didn't really care very much about his well-being, but it seemed so strange that he'd be calling me that I wondered whether he was being held at gunpoint in his office and mine was the only number he could see from an open faculty directory on his desk. I imagined his unruly gray hair getting more unruly from stress, transforming into an Einstein coif. I pictured the armpit stains spreading on his light green polyester-blend short sleeve button-down.

"Well," Dale said, "there's a bit of an urgent situation."

"Yes?" I said, feeling a spark of excitement. I was ready to drive to the college, burst into Grimwell Hall holding a shovel, prepared to beat any intruders over the head. Or, if not that, I was ready to summon Public Safety on Dale's behalf.

"Sort of an emergency," Dale said.

"Yes, yes?"

"You know Kayla Cooper?"

I knew Kayla Cooper. She was a senior English and business double major, philosophy and prelaw double minor. She loved telling everyone how many majors and minors she had, and she loved telling everyone, especially her professors, how she was such an incredibly busy person. She was a know-it-all, blathering on all the time, espousing her usually incorrect theories. I imagined her holding Dale hostage, demanding he change her grade from a B to an A.

"What's she done to you?" I said. "Do you need me to come over to the office?"

"Done to me? No, no, you stay put. I'm at home, not at school. It's just a matter of this conference that she'd like to go to, and I was wondering if you'd chaperone. The deadline for registering is today. Kayla just emailed me about it. The College requires a faculty member to accompany students on all trips."

I felt deflated. This was decidedly unexciting.

"The conference is in Vermont, so only a little more than an hour away, an easy trip. Next Thursday and Friday. It's for editors of undergraduate literary journals. Kayla wants to go with Hunter Leoni. They're both on the editorial board of *Cumulus.*"

"I know that," I said. I was their faculty advisor. Kayla and her crew were running the literary journal to the ground because Kayla, the editor in chief, always claimed she was too busy to organize any events or solicit work from students in my creative writing classes. Therefore, when the journal came out in May each year, it featured about five of Kayla's mediocre stories, a handful of her equally mediocre poems, and a dozen mediocre stories and poems from other members of the staff of *Cumulus*.

"The administration would really love it if you'd do it. They're encouraging us to do things with our students outside the classroom."

"'Doing things with our students outside the classroom' seems problematically vague, Dale."

He ignored my comment, which is what he generally did when I tried to stir up trouble. "Would you be able to drive a van? I mean, with the students in it. You'd have to go through campus van driver training first, but you've got a week, so that could be accomplished."

I didn't want to drive a van. I didn't want Kayla sitting in the passenger seat pulling up Google Maps on her phone and barking directions at me. I didn't want Hunter Leoni slumped in the back taking a nap, like he did during most days of my Introduction to Creative Writing class. I wanted to drive my own car and be free to come and go as I pleased. "I had a bad van experience in college," I said, even though this wasn't true. But the man at the dog park had been quick to believe my lie about dog breeds, so I figured I'd try lying to Dale. "I was in this band and we were touring and . . . bad things happened." I would have tried harder with the lie if it had been anyone else besides Dale, but he had very little imagination, which made him the ideal administrator. I imagined him whistling cheerfully over Excel spreadsheets as he figured out our course and classroom assignments each semester. He liked charts, numbers, and order, and sometimes I wondered whether he'd have been better off in the Accounting Department than the English Department. Plus, he wouldn't want to hear a more elaborate lie. He was always quick to depart the room if anyone, especially a woman, revealed anything about their personal lives, which reminded me of a series of male gym teachers I'd had throughout middle and high school who would excuse any girl from gym who simply clutched her midsection and said, "Cramps."

"All right, no van then," said Dale. "I think Kayla has her own car. So, yes, you'll chaperone them? You go in your car, they go in Kayla's car?"

"Fine," I said. "But this means I have to cancel my classes and shift around all the assignments on my syllabi."

"Excellent. But there's one more crinkle in the plan. We currently don't have funding for the students to attend. Or for you to attend. Will you put everything on your credit card? You need to book the hotel today if you want to get the conference rate. And," he coughed, "you need to book two rooms for the students. We cannot have a girl and a boy sharing a room. We'll figure out reimbursement later. I'll try to squeeze some money from a variety of sources on campus."

"I am not independently wealthy," I said. "Also, I believe we're supposed to refer to them as women and men, not girls and boys. And why should I be working extra hard to make the administration happy when they cut our salaries by 7 percent this year?"

"Yes, Amy, I know," said Dale. He sighed for a long time and so loudly that Gunner, who'd been resting at my feet, raised his head, alert. "We'll figure out a way to get you reimbursed, but for now the school can't front the money."

"If the school won't pay me back, will you?" It was unfair to ask, I knew, and I was talking to him more as if he were my father than my department chair, but Dale always brought out the insolent child in me.

"We'll figure something out."

"But I can't leave my dogs alone overnight. Will you watch them?"

"Oh, I, well, I suppose I . . ."

"I think it's a fair trade: two dogs for two students. You have a huge house. And a huge backyard. You could just leave them in your backyard and then have your cleaning lady pick up the poop after I come retrieve them."

Every year Dale threw a department holiday party at his house. His mansion. The first year I'd been invited to the party, I'd stood there gaping in the living room, looking at the spiral staircase that led upstairs, and Rhia Sethi, our postcolonialist, sidled up to me and whispered, "His wife's a lawyer. And he's got family money."

"Why is he teaching, then?" I asked.

Rhia took a sip of chardonnay and shrugged. "This is the question we all ask."

I heard Dale clear his throat on the other end of the line. "I could walk them," he said.

"Walk who?"

"The dogs. Your dogs. I had a dog as a boy. Roger. He was a basset hound. He was slow and too fat, but I loved that old boy. And I'd like to think he loved me too."

I didn't know what to say. This was more than Dale had ever shared about his life with me. Even during the Christmas parties, his wife was always away, supposedly on business trips, and although there was artwork on the walls of the living room—the only room we were allowed to be in—it didn't contain any photographs of Dale or his family. Most of the artwork was paintings of trees. I didn't even know if Dale had children, which is maybe something one should know about someone you've worked with for four years.

"Dale, you don't have any pets right now, do you?" I asked.

"Just a hedgehog," he said. "But he won't bother your dogs at all. I'll keep him in the bedroom."

I couldn't deal with imagining Dale a) in his bedroom, or b) with a hedgehog on his nightstand. And so the only thing I could think of saying before I slammed down the phone was, "I am going to be so fucking pissed if one of my dogs eats your hedgehog and then I have to pay for a trip to the vet on top of everything else."

The first day of the conference was fine. Or as fine as a conference like that could be. It consisted of seven hours of presentations by undergraduates. Much of the day involved said undergraduates trying to remember their passwords so they could get into Google Drive and search for their slideshows. Often they would spend three or four minutes testing out a variety of passwords on the computer at the front of the room before they hit upon the right one. Most of the presentations were boring and bumbling. There was a lot of mumbling and squinting while reading notes off phones, and there was one boy who presented while balanced on one leg like a flamingo, crutches tucked into both armpits. The grimy cast on the boy's leg was covered in signatures, and of course the cast reminded me of Vincent's broken arm. I had asked if I could sign his cast after we'd gotten home from the hospital and he'd said, "I'm not a child. I don't intend to go around collecting signatures."

I told Vincent that when I was twelve I'd broken my arm falling off a boulder I'd scrambled up onto during a Girl Scout camping trip despite my troop leader's warnings that the boulder was slippery. "You should have smelled the cast when it came off after six weeks," I said.

Vincent shook his head. "Well, that's how we're different, isn't it? You broke your arm because of your own lack of discipline and carelessness."

I knew he blamed me for the broken arm. I had talked him into going skydiving with the idea that it might somehow save our marriage, might scare our hearts into beating hard and wildly, might wake us up in some way. I was bored with everything, bored with us, with our lives, with my job, with the novel I'd been writing for seven years that still wasn't finished or right in any way. We'd been married for six years by that point, and people had given up on asking us if we were going to have children. It was a possibility, but a possibility for the distant future was how I always thought of it. Vincent's accusations that I was irresponsible and never took anything seriously were not untrue, and I kept thinking, year after year, that I wasn't quite ready for children, and then we were both thirty-seven and it had become more of a time-sensitive issue. But I told Vincent that before we could even consider children seriously, we had to do all the fun things I'd always wanted to do, and Vincent had said, "I think your idea of fun is very different from mine," yet he'd agreed to go skydiving with me.

"If we die," I told him in the plane, "it's good that we'll have left no one behind."

"We have two dogs," Vincent said, and I realized I'd completely forgotten about Gunner and Rufus.

Something went wrong with Vincent's landing, not something with the parachute but something with Vincent freaking out and flinging himself onto the ground after his feet touched land, and that's how his arm broke. At the hospital we sat in a dark room and he pointed to the X-ray, glowing in an X-ray illuminator, of his broken ulna and radius and said, "It's a metaphor for us. Broken."

"Metaphors are my territory," I said. "Insurance brokers don't get to use metaphors." I smiled at Vincent, but he didn't smile back. He'd wanted me to grow up, and it hadn't happened, and he said he was uncertain I ever would.

I was struck by the sound of pencils scratching wildly on notebook paper, and I turned to look at Kayla and Hunter, who were scribbling notes on what the boy with the crutches was presenting on, something about creative nonfiction and how you have to make sure people aren't lying in their essays before you publish them or you could get in big trouble as editors. On the screen was a white slide with only the word TRUTH typed on it in large, bold black letters. I'd never had Kayla in class because she believed she already knew everything she needed to know about creative writing, but I'd also never seen Hunter so alert in any of my classes and I had never, not once, seen him take notes, never imagined he could write so quickly and vigorously. The boy on crutches said, "Raise your hand if your school offers creative nonfiction classes," and Kayla and Hunter sat there, hands not raised, pencils poised to jot down the next thing the boy had to say about creative nonfiction. "Raise your hands," I hissed. "*I* teach creative nonfiction.

Every fall!" Dutifully, they raised their hands, although the looks on their faces showed they were dubious.

Because Kayla was a senior and Hunter a sophomore, she treated him like a baby, insisting he report his whereabouts to her. During a break from the endless slideshows, Hunter stood up, and Kayla said, "Where are you going?"

"Bathroom?"

"Well, you just make sure you're back before the next presentation begins," Kayla said, and Hunter nodded as though it were perfectly acceptable for Kayla to bark at him as if he were her toddler. "Call me if you get lost," said Kayla, her hand over her iPhone.

"God, Kayla," I said, after Hunter left, "the bathroom is right down the hall."

Kayla sighed. "In case you hadn't noticed, Dr. Miller, Hunter is kind of an oaf."

I had, in fact, noticed that Hunter was somewhat oafish. He was one of those boys who'd grown too big too fast; he was unkempt throughout much of the semester, letting his hair and beard grow until he went home for breaks and was likely forced by his mother to clean himself up. Overall, he presented much like a Saint Bernard, oafish and large, fuzzy but pleasant.

"It doesn't seem nice to call your coeditor an oaf," I said.

"But, Dr. Miller, doesn't he remind you of Shrek? I mean, Dr. Miller, just a little bit?"

I hated the Dr. Miller, Dr. Miller, Dr. Miller business with Kayla. If she paid any attention to anything she'd know I had an MFA, not a PhD. I hated the repetition of my name with an incorrect title attached to it. I was sure she'd read about repeating names in some handbook for junior businesspeople, something about how to ingratiate yourself to people by saying their names over and over.

"I'm sorry, Kayla, but I don't know who Shrek is," I lied. "Is that some football player?"

"Oh, Dr. Miller, no, not at all. He's a movie star."

"Like Brad Pitt?"

"No!" Kayla said, a little too loudly, and some of the non-bathroom goers and nonsmokers who stayed in the room during the break turned to look at her. "Dr. Miller, Brad Pitt is handsome. And Hunter? Do you think Hunter is handsome?"

"Legally, I'm not allowed to answer that question," I said.

"I'm not sure that's true," said Kayla. "You know I'm pre-law, right? Along with my philosophy minor and my English and business majors."

"Well, I'm not a lawyer, but I'm just saying you've still got a lot to learn in those prelaw classes. Wait, do *you* think Hunter is handsome?"

"Oh, I," Kayla said and stopped speaking and her face flushed red.

I saved her from answering by saying, "Look, Shrek's coming back, so let's cease and desist with this conversation."

At lunch some of the other professors who were at the conference gathered together and others sat with their students, but I wanted to do neither, so I took a paper bag labeled TURKEY CLUB off a table with dozens of bagged lunches and wandered around the campus where the conference was being held until I found a bench behind the art building. Inside the building a handful of students wearing safety glasses were using loud circular saws to cut pieces of wood. I liked the noise, the constant raucous whirring that drowned everything else out.

I'd told Kayla and Hunter I needed to make a phone call, but that wasn't true. In the past I would have called Vincent, whispered to him about Kayla and Hunter, the poorly made slideshows, the word TRUTH hovering over the boy on crutches, but now I could no longer call him to jabber on about unimportant matters. He didn't want to hear from me. I could call and ask how his arm was doing, but I didn't want to bring that up either. When I had agreed to the divorce I knew there'd be an empty space in our home, but I didn't think of the times when I would want to call or email Vincent and have to stop myself. I missed Vincent most, it seemed, outside of the house, when I wanted to let him know how the day went, to run some sort of silliness or frustration by him.

I wanted to talk to someone, so I called Dale's office at school. "Yes?" he said.

"It's Amy. I'm calling about the dogs. Just checking in."

"I have Rufus with me," said Dale. He laughed, spoke away from the mouthpiece of the phone, and I thought I heard him say, "Good boy, who's a good, good boy?" I couldn't be sure, though, because of the noise of the saws.

"You have Rufus in the office?"

"He's tiny. No one cares. The students like playing with him."

"We're not supposed to have pets in the office. If I knew that wasn't a rule that actually had to be followed I'd have brought in Gunner and kept him under my desk and used him to warm my feet. As you know, the heat doesn't work in my office."

"Gunner is too big," said Dale. "Come here, baby."

"Where is Gunner? And did you just call Rufus '*baby*'?"

"Gunner's at home. Safe and sound. What breed is Rufus, by the way?"

"A blue marmoset schnauzer."

Dale was silent for a second. Then I thought I heard him typing something. "There's no such thing, Amy."

"No, you're right. He's the result of the coupling of a Chihuahua and a hedgehog."

"You should know that both dogs have behaved impeccably around Lord Byron."

Again, I wished I could call Vincent, to tell him that not only did Dale own a hedgehog, but he'd also named it Lord Byron.

"What's going on there?" said Dale. "What's all that racket? I can barely hear you."

"Oh, that. We're just having a shredding party. We're taking all the literary journals the students brought and we're shredding them. Because they're terrible."

"All of them?" said Dale. "That's hard to believe."

"Yes, all of them. We're using this conference as a fresh start. A do-over for *Cumulus*. It needs to be built again from the ground up."

"Well, that's good. So this conference worked out. Aren't you glad you went?"

"Oh, so glad," I said. "So, so glad for this new and fresh start."

I told Kayla and Hunter I would drive to dinner, so I picked them up in the lobby of our hotel and walked to my car, a fifteen-year-old Toyota. I had to chauffer the students to dinner, pay for food and beverages, and hope for reimbursement at some point. I watched Kayla closely as she got in the passenger seat. She seemed disappointed, as if she'd expected something much nicer. Hunter squeezed himself into the backseat, and the roof squished his puffy hair.

It was dark already and it was raining. I got lost getting to the small downtown, looped onto a highway that took me out of Vermont and back into upstate New York for a few miles, then when I got back off the highway I found myself on a dirt road, and there was fog floating near the ground. A few minutes down the road we crossed over a red covered bridge. From the backseat Hunter said, "This kind of feels like being in a horror movie," but he said it with such a flat affect that I was unsure if he was excited or upset.

There were only a few restaurants in the two-block downtown, so I picked a brewery and only after we were seated did I realize that I shouldn't order a beer since the college wouldn't reimburse for alcohol, plus Kayla was old enough to order alcohol and the last thing I wanted to do was pay for her beer. Kayla ordered the lobster mac and cheese, the most expensive item on the menu, while Hunter and I both ordered moderately priced sandwiches. I still didn't know if I would get money back for this outing and I was already out more than eight hundred dollars for the registration fees and hotel for the three of us.

"Would anyone mind if I ordered dessert?" Kayla asked when we'd finished our meals.

"That's fine, whatever," said Hunter.

While we waited for Kayla's baked Alaska to arrive, she leaned toward me and said, "Dr. Miller, I have an important matter to discuss with you."

I looked at the labels on the large silver tanks of beer that were brewing behind Kayla's head. IPA. Porter. Stout. Pumpkin seasonal. I wanted a beer but I knew if I ordered one, Kayla would order one too, and I was still committed to keeping her meal under fifty dollars.

"We were thinking of amending our club constitution to say that we won't accept any materials that include use of illegal substances, sexual situations, or cursing," Kayla said.

"Why would you do that?" I asked.

"Because the college has an honor code."

"The honor code just means you're not supposed to cheat on take-home exams and you're not supposed to talk about your grades," I said. "It has nothing to do with the literary journal."

"Yes, but I just don't agree with inappropriate material."

"Maybe you don't personally agree, but have you considered that what you want to do is censorship?"

"I wouldn't exactly call it censorship."

"Then what would you call it?"

"I would call it being selective."

"Hunter, what do you think?" I asked.

"Oh," said Hunter slowly, his eyes moving to Kayla's face. She squinted and her lips drew into a rigid line. Her hand twitched and I thought she might hit Hunter if he answered incorrectly. "Well," said Hunter, "I guess I can see both sides of the argument."

"People use drugs. They have sex. They curse," I said, and Kayla's eyes opened wide.

"No," she said.

"No? You're denying that people engage in these activities?"

"I'm not. I'm just saying I don't want to read about these activities. Look, I know where you stand on this, but do you think you could ask the president what he thinks I should do?"

"The president of what?"

"The college. I'm sure he has some thoughts on this. Could you imagine what would happen if he read the literary journal and saw something scandalous?"

"Actually, I can't imagine the president reading the literary journal at all. I would put good money on him not even knowing of the journal's existence."

"No," Kayla said again. "I'm certain he reads it. I brought a copy to his house last May. His wife was in the front yard gardening, and I gave her the journal and asked her to give it to him. She said she'd make sure he got it."

"I didn't think students were supposed to go bother the president and his family at home," said Hunter.

"Well, yes, students shouldn't, but the editor in chief of the literary journal is a completely different matter," said Kayla, and she shoved a large spoonful of baked Alaska into her mouth.

After I dropped Kayla and Hunter off at the hotel after dinner, I decided I needed wine. By this point alcohol was a need, not just a want. There was a supermarket down the street from the hotel and I picked up two tiny boxes of malbec. These boxes had twist tops, which meant I could dispense with a corkscrew—which I had not packed—and drink directly out of the box.

It was only 7:00 p.m., and I didn't want to go back to the hotel and be alone for the hours until I fell asleep. Besides academic conferences, I was never in hotels alone; hotels reminded me of taking trips with Vincent. I liked going on vacation with him, getting away from everything, seeing new things. Vincent was a planner, loved getting maps and highlighting the path we'd travel with a yellow marker, even though we could leave the directions up to the GPS on our phones. He studied too much before we went anywhere, memorizing the ten-day forecast, reading the Yelp reviews of all the most popular restaurants in the area, studying the topography. Throughout these trips he'd bust out facts and statistics about wherever we were visiting, and I would tune him out. Later, I'd inevitably ask him about something he'd already talked about, and he'd say, "Do you ever listen to anything I have to say?" His facts used to annoy me, but now I wished he were beside me in the grocery store, telling me which boxed wine *Consumer Reports* had rated as the best, coming up with a plan for the evening, spouting off facts about the elevation of the Green Mountains.

I walked up and down the aisles of the supermarket, dragging out the time before returning to my room. As I walked, I got an idea. In one aisle I grabbed a box of Gobstoppers. In the next aisle there were cheap toys, and I saw a treasure hunting kit, which included a map, a compass, and a magnifying glass. I put the kit in my cart. Then I saw a basket of small plastic moose and placed half a dozen in my cart too.

I returned to my hotel room, drank one box of wine, drove to the covered bridge we'd driven over earlier, set things up, and returned to knock on Kayla's door. She opened the door dressed in flannel pajamas with poodles on them and fluffy white slippers.

"You're going to sleep already?" I said. "It's not even nine."

"The day was exhausting, Dr. Miller." She stood in the doorway blinking at me.

"Do you and Hunter want to go do something with me?"

"Hunter's FaceTiming with his girlfriend right now."

"Hunter has a girlfriend?"

"I know, can you believe it, Dr. Miller?"

"Well, didn't Shrek eventually find a girlfriend?"

"I thought you didn't know who Shrek was."

"Listen, do you want to go?"

"Go where?"

"On an adventure."

"I don't know, Dr. Miller. We have to get up early tomorrow for the conference."

"Live a little, Kayla."

"I'm in my pajamas. It's not appropriate to go outside in pajamas."

"So change."

"I have homework to do. I have a double major and two minors."

"Why do that to yourself? Why sign up for so much?"

Kayla shrugged. Then she said, "I need to make everyone happy. My mom works for Goldman Sachs and wants me to go to business school after I graduate. My dad's a lawyer. He was an English major, though, and he said lawyers should be able to read and write well. Everyone wants me to follow in their footsteps."

"And what do you want to do?"

Kayla paused. "I have no idea," she said. "I don't know what I'm going to do or what I'm good at. And I'm graduating in a semester. Do you have any advice for me?"

"You'll figure it out," I said, but I knew it was one of the worst things to say. This was the kind of thing clueless adults who didn't remember being young and confused and unsure of the future said to younger people. "So are you coming or what?"

Kayla stared at me for a few seconds. I knew that if nothing else she was curious. Plus, if she came, the next day she could boast to Hunter she'd done something he hadn't done, that she'd been invited out by a professor. "All right, Dr. Miller," she said. "I'll join you."

In the car, Kayla asked where we were going. The rain was coming down harder, and one of the wipers squealed each time it passed over the windshield.

"Nightclub," I said.

"Oh, no, really? I've never been to one. And I don't think I'm dressed for it. Oh, Dr. Miller, no, we can't do this."

I laughed. "Kayla, look around. What do you see?"

"Trees. Woods."

"Exactly. I was kidding about the nightclub. I don't think there's one within fifty miles. Just calm down." I reached into my pocket and extracted two Gobstoppers from a Ziploc bag I'd put them in earlier. I had originally brought the Ziploc to slip the hotel's TV remote into. It was something Vincent had always done because he said hotel remotes were some of the most germ-infested objects in the world, but I'd already picked up and used the remote and had forgotten to put the Ziploc over it when I'd remembered I had one in my suitcase. "Have one of these."

"What is that?"

"It'll calm you down. The street name is Ataraxia."

"Dr. Miller, I don't do drugs. And you shouldn't either, especially not while operating a motor vehicle. You know I'm going to have to tell Dr. Grommet about this when we get back."

"Take one, Kayla. Take the red one. It's for people who are really uptight. I'm having the green one since I'm already halfway mellow from drinking some wine earlier."

"Are you driving drunk?" Kayla said. "That's not safe, especially not on a rainy night."

I extended my hand with the red Gobstopper in it. Kayla took the Gobstopper, rolled it around her fingers, and smelled it. She stuck out her tongue and licked it.

"Dr. Miller, this is an Everlasting Gobstopper."

"Maybe," I said. "Or maybe it's just packaged to look and taste like a Gobstopper. Eat it and see what happens."

Kayla rolled down her window and threw the Gobstopper out.

"Great," I said. "Do you know how much that one Ataraxia cost?" I wondered if I could take Gobstoppers to the dog park and sell them to the hipster lumberjack or to suburban moms who wanted an escape from the drudgery of their daily lives, the monotony of cook, clean, bath time, bedtime, repeat.

"Dr. Miller, could you please take me back to the hotel? I don't want to be in this car with you in your compromised state."

"Ha! I'm just like one of those characters in the stories you want to censor, right? What's my next move? What's my next *crazed* move under the influence of a small box of wine?"

"Dr. Miller, I think you've lost your mind." Kayla grabbed the handle on the passenger side door. "How about you pull over and let me drive?"

"It's fine. We're here anyway." I stopped next to the covered bridge. Kayla took her phone out of her pocket.

"I don't have reception," she said.

"Don't worry about it. My phone isn't working out here either." I could tell she was panicked. I reached into my jacket pocket and withdrew the map from the treasure hunting kit I'd gotten at the supermarket. "I found this," I said. "In the tote bag I got at the conference. I think someone wanted to let me know there was treasure out here."

I'd taken the map and wrinkled it up and had drawn a few landmarks on it that I'd seen on my drive, including the covered bridge. I'd ripped off part of the map that showed an Egyptian pyramid and claimed there was a "tomb of jewels" inside.

"This is a toy," said Kayla.

"*Is it?*" I said. "Or is it a map to treasure?"

"Why would they put a map to treasure in your tote bag only, Dr. Miller?"

"Sometimes our job isn't to ask why," I said. "Sometimes our job is to seek out adventure when it's been laid before us."

"Dr. Miller, I think you're drunk."

"Stop it, just stop it, would you, with the Dr. Millers? Enough. Can you just call me Amy?" The car was beginning to fog up from our breath.

"I can't call you by your first name. You're a professor."

"Then just call me 'Hey, you' if you need me but stop with the constant Dr. Millers, okay? Miller's my husband—my ex-husband's—last name. I just can't stand hearing it come out of your mouth every five seconds." I unbuckled my seatbelt.

"Oh," Kayla said. "I didn't know. You're still wearing your ring."

"Let's get out of the car," I said. "There's an X on the treasure map at this bridge."

I led Kayla inside the covered bridge. Our footsteps echoed in the damp darkness. It felt cooler inside the bridge than it had outside. I could barely see anything, just Kayla's shadowy silhouette.

Kayla pulled a small flashlight out of the pocket of her jacket and shone it around the bridge.

"You're impressively prepared," I said.

"I'm a Girl Scout," Kayla said. "I haven't been able to keep up this year, but maybe after I graduate."

"Yeah, maybe you can be a full-time adult Girl Scout after graduation," I said. "Can you get a badge for having the most majors and minors of any Girl Scout?"

She glared at me. "This is totally creepy. I wish Hunter were here. He could at least defend me in case you go completely off the rail."

"I was once a Girl Scout," I said.

"Apparently you learned nothing about being a good citizen," Kayla said.

I laughed. I wondered if Kayla really thought I was going to do something horrible to her, maybe kill her and bury her body under the bridge. I wondered if the thought that these were the last moments of her life had made her bolder than usual.

I put two Gobstoppers in my mouth and let them clack against my teeth. I held out the bag to Kayla, but she shook her head. "Hey, are you into Hunter?" I asked.

"No, I, no, I mean, he's nice and all but he has a girlfriend."

"And if he didn't? You'd go for him?"

"It's not exactly that simple in matters of the heart."

"No, it's not. You're right about that."

"The thing is, Hunter would never go for me. His girlfriend is gorgeous. And look at me."

"Oh, Kayla, you're . . ?" I swept a hand toward her, taking in her long dark hair, her black North Face jacket, her gray sweatpants with the college's logo printed up the side, her Uggs. She looked like thousands of other twenty-one-year-old girls. There was nothing that would make her stand out, nothing bad, really, besides her personality.

"See, now this is where you should be lying. I believe it's called a white lie and you tell me that I'm not an ogre and it wouldn't be impossible for Hunter to like me."

"I was just distracted," I said. "Just thinking of how Hunter could find himself a gorgeous girlfriend."

Kayla shrugged. "He's easy to boss around. Some women find that attractive."

She stomped to the side of the covered bridge, her steps reverberating. She shined her flashlight up a horizontal beam then reached up. She pulled down a moose. She stepped a few feet away and pulled down another. She kept going until she'd pulled down all six moose I'd purchased earlier in the evening.

"The meese are a clue to treasure?" said Kayla.

"Is meese the plural of moose? Not moose? Like shrimp is the plural of shrimp?"

"I'm certain it's meese," Kayla said.

"I think the moose or meese *are* the treasure."

Kayla examined a moose under the beam of her flashlight, held it up close to her face in the darkness. "Did you come out here after dinner to put the meese here? Why would you do that? Don't you have papers to grade or something?"

"I have plenty to do."

"And instead you do this? What's wrong with you?" She put the moose on the ground, lined up in a neat row near the side of the bridge, so if any cars drove over the bridge they would not get crushed. I could hear rain falling outside. Kayla's hair had frizzed from the moisture, and her words came out with small puffs of smoke.

"I don't know what's wrong with me," I said, and I really didn't. But I was starting to think that maybe Vincent was right, in some ways at least, about my needing to grow up, to take things more seriously. How had I found myself on this dark bridge on a cold night with Kayla Cooper? What was I hoping to accomplish? I was like that hipster lumberjack holding the Pomeranian in the dog park: someone ridiculous with no good reason to be where I was.

"I was supposed to call my parents tonight. To let them know I'm okay. They would freak out if they knew I was in the middle of the woods," Kayla said.

I thought it was nice, important, to have someone to report in to, someone who cared about your whereabouts. In just a few months Kayla would be thrust into the world, and no matter how many majors and minors she had, they wouldn't protect her from how difficult real life could be. Nothing in textbooks and classrooms really prepared people for how to live once you were on your own.

"Let's go," I said. "You want the moose?"

Kayla shook her head, shined her flashlight beam over them one more time, then clomped toward the car and impatiently pulled the door handle.

In the car Kayla shivered, wrapped her arms around her torso. I turned up the heat and we drove away from the bridge and headed back toward paved roads. My left arm, the one that I'd broken all those years ago, bothered me and I steered with only my right hand. My left arm got sore when it rained hard, when it was damp, as though the bones could remember how once they'd been shattered. I thought about Vincent and his still-healing arm, and I hoped this last surgery would work, that his bones would grow together correctly. I thought about Dale playing with our dogs—no, my dogs—maybe with them curled up on his bed, warming his feet. I wondered if the dogs would want to come home to me after all the attention Dale had given them, after Rufus's field trips to campus.

"So all of that, it was really a wild goose chase," said Kayla. She fidgeted with the zipper on her jacket, zipping it up and down, up and down. "A waste of time. Do you know how much homework I have to do?"

The first thing that popped into my mind was wild *moose* chase, but I didn't say it out loud, didn't say, "No, Kayla, not a wild goose chase. We went on a wild *moose* chase." Instead, I said something else, something I almost never said, had not ever said to Vincent in the years we were married. Instead, I said, "I'm sorry."

AQUATICS

Meredith unfurled her towel on the warm concrete next to the pool. She settled near the wooden fence in a shadowy spot none of the sunbathers wanted. It was the middle of July, but it was her first time at the pool that summer, and she wiggled her pale toes as she extended her legs. In June, her friend Ellie had been around. They'd spent the weeks after school ended trying to summon ghosts on Ellie's Ouija board; writing stories about female spies; creating rules for Megagame, which consisted of Monopoly, Clue, and Life boards taped together; and trying to sound out the melody lines to Whitney Houston's songs on their clarinets. But now Ellie was gone, at horseback riding camp for the next six weeks.

Meredith watched three girls from her class, who dangled their feet into the deep end of the pool. Jessie, Tiffany, and Cori all wore bikinis. They cheered when Chris Chester dove, and they cheered even harder when his head popped up and he spat out a spray of water. Chris looked different from how he'd looked when the school year ended. He was tanned and seemed taller, bigger. His hair was longer, curling under his ears, and lighter, too, bleached by the sun. Meredith pulled her feet in and sat cross-legged, making her navy blue Speedo swimsuit feel tight. She pulled it away from her body, and it snapped back hard, like a hand slapping her belly.

Earlier that day, when Meredith was swimming, Cori had floated over to her and said, "Are you on a swim team or something?" Cori treaded water, and her hands flashed in front of Meredith. Cori's fingernails were painted bright purple. For a moment Meredith had been flattered; maybe Cori had noticed how quickly she'd swum from one end of the pool to the other. Meredith shook her head, and Cori said, "Oh, I just thought maybe you were on a team because of your swimsuit."

"My swimsuit?"

"It's like . . . official or something. I just thought only real swimmers wore one-piece Speedos."

Meredith felt her face burn as she treaded water. The lifeguards blew their whistles and shouted, "Adult swim!" Meredith climbed out of the pool and Cori followed and stood next to her. Cori's stomach was flat, and she stood so her back was arched and her small breasts were pushed out in her bikini top.

"Hey, Meredith? How come you haven't been at the pool this summer?" Cori said. Meredith wished Cori would call her Merry, the way she used to. Cori was the only person in the world who used that nickname.

Meredith shrugged. "I was busy."

"Right," Cori said, as if she didn't believe Meredith, and she joined Tiffany and Jessie, who were flat on their bellies on their towels. All three bent their heads together and giggled, and Meredith wondered what secret had passed between them. In second grade Cori had told Meredith her full name was Coriander, but Meredith wasn't allowed to share that secret with anyone. Cori hated the name so much that she insisted her mother call each of her teachers before the school year started and ask them not to read her full name out loud from the roster when taking attendance. "My parents are hippies," Cori told Meredith when they first met, and Meredith asked what hippies were. "I can't really explain. They just say all the time that they are," Cori said. "That's why they named me after a spice."

When Meredith went to play at Cori's house she understood better what hippies meant. Cori's father was a musician and her mother was a painter. In their living room window, the one facing out to the street, was a sign that read "War Is Not the Answer." They had four cats and three dogs. Meredith's family had no pets because both of her parents were allergic to pet dander. Cori's parents were vegetarians, and on some nights when Meredith stayed for dinner Cori's mother made a loaf out of nuts and sunflower seeds and brown rice. Sometimes Cori's father would play the guitar and they'd sing along with him. Meredith learned all the words to "This Land Is Your Land" from Cori's father. Last year Cori decided her father and his guitar were stupid, and she refused to sing with him anymore.

In the past year Cori had decided that most everything was stupid, including Meredith. She now acted bored around Meredith and no longer invited her to her house. Meredith had loved going to Cori's house because it was so different from her own home with her mother's excessive rules and her father's constant reminders that if she did not get good grades she wouldn't get into a good college and then wouldn't be accepted into a top law school. He was certain she'd become a lawyer and would join his firm, but he never asked her if she actually wanted to be a lawyer. She thought she might want to be a veterinarian but she had not told her parents this.

Before coming to the pool, Meredith had argued with her mother. She wanted to take the bus to the pool, but her mother insisted on dropping her off. "But it's the same bus I took to school every day for six years!" Meredith said. The only difference was that instead of dropping its passengers off at the elementary school, it dropped them off at the town pool. "I could come sit with you at the pool for a while," her mother said. "I know you're lonely with Ellie out of town." Meredith argued that she wanted to take the bus and she wanted to be alone. She would be in junior high in the fall; it was time her mother learned to trust her. Finally her mother agreed to let her take the bus by herself.

Chris Chester dove again then shook water out of his hair when he scrambled out of the pool. He joined the three girls from Meredith's class, who were now sitting next to two boys: Mark Geller, who was also in Meredith's grade, and a boy in yellow swim trunks that Meredith did not know. The boy Meredith didn't know held a small plastic cooler, the kind her mother packed in their car's trunk for when she bought fancy cheeses from the gourmet market. The boy set the cooler down next to the three girls and sat on it as if it were a stool. Mark emptied a red paper cup that said "Coca-Cola" on its side onto Jessie, and ice cubes tumbled out. Jessie shrieked and jumped up to chase Mark. Mark hooted like an owl, and Jessie screamed, "I'm going to kill you!," but she had a smile on her face, and Tiffany and Cori laughed. Cori sat behind Tiffany and braided her hair, then twisted it and wrapped it around the top of Tiffany's head. It looked like a crown.

Meredith plucked her bathing suit away from her belly again and listened to the thwack it made when it contracted back. She reached into her tote bag and took out *The Diary of Anne Frank*, which was one of her assigned summer reading books. She tried to read but couldn't concentrate. She stared at the words on the page and told herself to always remember that her life would never be as bad as Anne Frank's. From behind her open book, she watched Cori, Tiffany, Jessie, and the three boys, who were now crowded around a wooden picnic table near the snack stand. The boys were eating from a large plate of crinkle-cut fries, shoving three or four fries into their mouths at once. The boy with the yellow shorts picked up a squeeze bottle of ketchup and squirted a thin stream onto Cori's shoulder.

"Oh my God!" shouted Cori, and she grabbed the bottle from the boy and squeezed ketchup into his hair. Jessie and Tiffany laughed hard. The boy with the yellow shorts moved to Cori's side of the table and enveloped her in his arms, trying to pry the ketchup bottle from her.

Was this what Cori now thought was fun? Until a year ago, one of Meredith and Cori's favorite activities had been writing plays together. They would create costumes and act out all the roles, and Cori's parents were always willing to be the audience. Meredith and Cori had laughed until they could barely breathe as they performed the plays, forgetting their lines, taking too long for costume changes. "Why do you always want to do such babyish things?" Cori asked the last time Meredith had gone to her house and suggested writing a new play. All Cori wanted to do now was go to the mall and look at earrings at Claire's.

"Stop it," said a lifeguard, who grabbed the ketchup bottle out of Cori's hands. "Move," the lifeguard said, and she marched Cori and the boy to the outdoor showers and told them to rinse the ketchup off. The lifeguard was wearing the same kind of swimsuit Meredith wore, a one-piece Speedo, but hers was red.

Whistles blew again, meaning adult swim was over, and the lifeguards who surrounded the pool shouted, "All swim!" Old women in bathing caps and swimsuits that had little skirts attached hauled themselves out of the pool. Meredith looked at the thick blue veins on one woman's legs. Then she stood, felt her swimsuit in the back to make sure it still fully covered her butt, and walked to the pool. She stepped into the shallow end and sank to the bottom and let the cold water wash over her.

After a few seconds the water no longer felt chilly, and she bobbed to the surface. The pool was nearly empty. Only a few children were in the shallowest part, their arms in inflated floaties. It was quiet, no more shouting or giggling or shrieking or whistles blowing when kids ran instead of walked near the pool. It was almost dinnertime, and many of the families had left. Meredith would have to leave soon because the last bus to depart the pool was at six. There was no one at the deep end, and Meredith took a long breath and dove beneath the water and glided to the end of the pool without coming up for a breath. She imagined she was the fastest woman in the world training for the Olympics, swimming in her private pool, one that had been built in her backyard for her to train in. When her palm touched the wall, she crested to the surface and drew in a deep breath. She heard giggling outside the pool. Cori and her friends were near the deep end, hunched over the cooler the boy in the yellow swim trunks had carried around all day. "I dare you," Cori said to the boy.

Meredith thought there might be beer in the cooler. She pushed her back against the side of the pool and felt the rough surface of the wall on her skin. She rested her arms on the ledge and caught her breath. How much trouble would the boy get into if he drank beer in front of the lifeguards?

"Now," said Jessie. "No one's here now. Do it."

"She's here," said Tiffany, and when Meredith swiveled her head, she saw that Tiffany was pointing at her.

"She doesn't matter," said Cori.

"I'm gone," said Meredith, but she said it so quietly that no one seemed to hear. She took a deep breath and sank and sank until she could feel the bumpy surface of the bottom of the pool on her fingertips. She thought of Ellie, then, and wondered how many new friends she had already made at horse camp. There was a disturbance in the water above her, and when she opened her eyes and tilted her head, she saw jellyfish, about two dozen translucent domes, drifting downward. She remembered learning in Life Science that a group of jellyfish in a small area was called a bloom, and she thought it was a perfect word to describe these jellyfish floating around her, unfurling like flowers in a time-lapse video. She could make out the blurry image of the boy in the yellow shorts, his opened ice chest held above the water. Her heart pumped in her ears, quick, hard thumps. She floated, as if in outer space, and watched as the jellyfish, illuminated by diamonds of sunlight above, pulsed. And then she felt a sting on her leg, and as she shot up she felt arms wrap around her, and then they were on the surface and the girl lifeguard, the one wearing the red Speedo, pushed Meredith out of the pool, and Meredith sat dripping and coughing up water onto the hot concrete near the edge of the pool.

Everyone else who'd been in the pool was now standing outside of it, staring, and one of the lifeguards, a teenager with dyed fluorescent orange hair, screamed at the boy in the yellow trunks, and the lifeguard who'd saved Meredith said, "Enough yelling, just go to the office and get me gloves, tweezers, and Benadryl," and Meredith looked down and saw a tentacle that had separated from a jellyfish was still attached to her leg, and as soon as she saw it she felt a stab of pain. She pulled in a deep, jagged breath. "Can you breathe?" asked the lifeguard, and Meredith nodded. Cori said, "You're supposed to pee on jellyfish stings," and the girl lifeguard shook her head and said, "Urine makes the sting hurt more."

"Were *you* going to pee on her?" Mark asked Cori, and he laughed. Three lifeguards were using nets on long poles to get the jellyfish out of the pool. A man with a gray mustache brought over two metal buckets and put one on each of the long sides of the pool. The lifeguards dropped jellyfish from their nets into the buckets.

"None of you move," the girl lifeguard said. "You're all in trouble." The lifeguard smoothed back the hair from Meredith's face. "You'll be okay," she said. She asked Meredith what her name was. The lifeguard said her name was Jane.

Meredith looked at Cori, Jessie, and Tiffany in their bikinis, their tanned knobby knees near her eye level. She looked up at their thin arms. She wondered if any of them would have been strong enough to push her out of the pool. "Later," Jane said, pointing up at the three girls and three boys who stood in a row over Meredith, "I'm going to get your names and I'm going to call your parents."

"My name is Scooby-Doo," said Mark, and the rest of the group laughed.

"It's not funny, none of this is. We're going to have to close the pool and drain it. And if Meredith has an allergic reaction to the sting, you're in for a world of trouble." Jane stood and walked in front of the boy with the yellow swim trunks. She was taller than he was by at least three inches. "Did you think about cruelty to animals?" she asked. "Taking the jellyfish from wherever you found them and throwing them into chlorinated water?"

The boy with the yellow trunks didn't say anything. Meredith's leg throbbed. She tried to catch Cori's eye, but Cori only looked back-and-forth between Tiffany and Jessie. Meredith wanted someone to apologize, to tell her that they hadn't seen her in the water, but then she remembered what Cori had said: *She doesn't matter.*

The orange-haired lifeguard returned from the office carrying supplies. Jane put on the rubber gloves and held the tweezers over the tentacle on Meredith's leg. Meredith's leg pulsed with pain. Jane looked up at the six figures looming above her. "What?" she said. "You think this is some sort of show?" She turned to the other lifeguard. "Can you take them to the office? Get their names and phone numbers. Call their parents."

Meredith thought of Cori's parents, the antiwar sign in their window, the songs Cori's father sang about taking care of the land and the animals. She knew they'd be disappointed in Cori.

"We're not going with you," said the boy in the yellow swim trunks. "And besides, I don't even live in New York. I'm just visiting my cousin," he said, pointing to Chris.

"And we're not telling you our names," said Cori.

Meredith tried once again to catch Cori's eye, but Cori still would not look at her. There were goosebumps on Cori's legs, and the white outline of flip-flops was visible on her bare tan feet. "I know all their names except for his," Meredith said, pointing to the boy in the yellow shorts.

"Don't," said Cori, and she finally looked at Meredith. She looked her right in the eyes, but Cori's eyes were hard, unkind. Meredith thought of the staring contests they used to have, how they'd try to sit still and look into each other's eyes, but one of them would always start laughing within a few seconds. Why had everything seemed so funny back then?

Meredith pointed at Cori and recited her phone number. She'd called that number so many times that she remembered exactly where her fingers went on the rotary phone, and she could dial without even looking down. The bells from the church down the street chimed, and Meredith knew it was six o'clock and she'd missed the last bus. She would have to call her mother, who would tell her she was irresponsible and she could not ride the bus alone again. "Please, don't, Merry," Cori whispered, but there was something that sounded wrong in Cori's voice, something lopsided and broken. Meredith had spent five years protecting Cori's secret as if it were something precious, but now she was done. "And her name," she said, looking at Jessie and Tiffany and then the three boys, "her name is Coriander."

LOST OR DAMAGED

It started with an innocent encounter. Olga Koslov was new in our school—and in the country—that winter. Olga could not figure out the change she needed in order to pay for lunch on her first day at school. She stared down at the American coins in her hand, and Gabe Winn helped her pluck out and pay the $1.47 she owed for chicken nuggets, peach slices, and a carton of milk. "Thank you," Olga said, and Gabe said, "Let me know anytime you need help." Olga must have taken that statement to be an invitation, so she followed him past the registers and to a table where they ate lunch together.

Long before the rest of us understood that the best way to be in the world is to be compassionate and kind, Gabe understood. His kindness likely was a result of the isolation and mockery he had suffered because he was fat and friendless in elementary school. In middle school Gabe began to shed weight, and by high school he was a real-life example of the ugly duckling turned swan. In high school he was nice to everyone, even the kids no one else spoke to.

My best friend at the time, Arielle Eaton, and I were seated in the cafeteria at a table near the registers. We watched Olga and Gabe closely. Arielle and I were fifteen that year, and we'd been friends since we were in the same nursery school class. In high school I was still a follower, glad Arielle was loud and bossy, so I would not have to make decisions if I trailed after her and did what she commanded. I was Arielle's dependable audience; I would laugh at her jokes, whether they were funny or not, and nod along to any assertion she made. I'd listen to her gossip on the phone and would ride my bike to her house with a backpack full of *YM* and *Sassy* magazines to flip through together when she was bored.

Arielle pointed to Olga, who was spearing a peach slice with a plastic fork, and said, "I've heard she's a slut." Arielle had been pining after Gabe for a year, but even though she was full of bravado and confidence, she was inexperienced with boys and shy around Gabe, barely able to speak. I knew she wanted Gabe to wake up one day and notice how smart and spectacular and beautiful she was, but that hadn't happened.

Olga wore corduroys, a wool sweater with images of sheep on it, and a turtleneck. She was dressed as my mother would have dressed me when I was in kindergarten, and it was difficult to picture her engaging in slutty behavior in a sweater festooned with sheep. "Who told you that?" I asked. It was too soon for Olga to have earned any sort of reputation, good or bad.

"I've just heard," snapped Arielle. I knew Arielle well enough to know she'd made up a lie about Olga because she was jealous that Olga and Gabe were sitting together.

"We could go sit with them," I said. "That way you can talk to Gabe too."

"I'm not sitting with Olaf."

"Olga," I said. Olga had been in our third period math class, and the teacher had introduced her to the rest of the class.

"Whatever. I heard her family got kicked out of Russia because her father was in the KGB."

"The KGB doesn't exist anymore," I said. "It was dissolved two years ago."

Arielle glared at me for a moment, but she did not respond. It was rare that I contradicted her, but I wanted to stop this lie before Arielle tried to tell it to anyone else. I told myself that by contradicting Arielle, I was making sure she would not look foolish when she inevitably began to spread her stories about Olga to the rest of the school.

"We are incredibly lucky to have a new student with us," declared our orchestra teacher, Mr. Himmelman, during sixth period that day. His hands were on Olga's shoulders, and he presented her to us, the rest of the string orchestra, as if she were a great gift. Olga stood holding her violin case, blushing. "She was first chair in her youth orchestra in Russia," Mr. Himmelman told us. "She auditioned for me earlier today, and she'll be an excellent addition to our violin section!"

I played the bass, and as I stood behind the cellos I watched anger simmer on Arielle's face. Arielle was the concertmistress, the first chair in the first violin section of our high school orchestra. This spot was usually reserved for a senior; Arielle was the first sophomore to be concertmistress. As a child, she'd won first place again and again at local, state, regional, and national music competitions. She hoped to attend Julliard after graduation. Everyone knew she was the best musician in our school, and it was assumed she would be concertmistress until she graduated.

I was a mediocre bass player. I had decided to play a stringed instrument so I could be in the orchestra with Arielle throughout high school. My mother suggested I take up the bass because she said it was an unusual instrument for girls to play and colleges would look upon this activity fondly. I went along with my mother's instrument choice because that's what I did back then; my most notable trait was my agreeableness.

"Let's do a little shifting," Mr. Himmelman said, and he used his baton to direct the members of the first violin section to move. Everyone took their sheet music, bows, and violins, and moved one seat back. Mr. Himmelman had decided Olga was to be first chair, which would also make her concertmistress. This would, of course, knock Arielle out of the position.

"Up, up, Arielle," Mr. Himmelman said, and Arielle looked at him, eyes wide, incredulous. "You move to second chair."

"But the solo in the Sibelius?" Arielle said. She had been given the solo in *Violin Concerto in D. Minor, Opus 47*, and I knew she spent three hours every evening practicing the difficult piece, recording herself on tape and playing it back to listen for mistakes. Sometimes I sat in her room and did homework while she practiced.

"You'll still play the solo in our winter concert. Don't worry," Mr. Himmelman said, and Arielle reluctantly moved one seat over.

Olga sat down, removed her violin from the case, and tuned it quietly. "Hello, I am Olga," she said to Arielle. "It is nice to meet you."

Arielle did not respond, her jaw clenched tightly. She raised her violin, and as we practiced the overture from the *Nutcracker Suite* she ground her bow violently into the strings, making several strands of hair on the bow break and wave angrily off the end.

As we walked home through the town park that afternoon, Arielle said, "Can you believe Olaf brought a Stradivarius to school?" We stopped by the pond in the middle of Sutter's Park and watched two little girls who were skating. Arielle and I used to skate on the pond when we were younger. Arielle had taken skating lessons throughout elementary school and had even won a few statewide figure skating competitions. I mostly wobbled on my skates, hoping not to fall on the ice, hoping not to break a bone. I'd watched Arielle compete on several occasions, breathless when she jumped and looped in the air, hoping she would land safely. In seventh grade she'd decided she couldn't be serious about both violin and skating and had given up skating.

"No way," I said. "A Stradivarius costs millions of dollars."

"Yeah, I know. I told you her dad was involved in sketchy business in Russia. She probably has like ten of them at home. Probably got them illegally."

"There are only a few hundred in the world. I doubt one person would have ten of them." I had read an article in one of my father's

Smithsonian magazines about the Stradivari family from Italy, the famous makers of stringed instruments in the seventeenth and eighteenth centuries. Even someone as good at violin as Olga would not be dragging a Stradivarius to high school. "If anything, it might be a reproduction or a really good fake," I said.

Arielle took a few steps down the bank next to the pond, then stood on the ice in her boots. She raised her hands over her head and spun around once.

"Do you miss ice skating?" I asked.

"I didn't," she said, "but now I think I might take it up again. I'll probably quit violin."

"Because Himmelman gave Olga first chair? You still have the solo."

"That was mortifying," she said. "He could have waited until next fall to shuffle the seats. He didn't have to do it right in front of everyone. And she's a freshman!"

"I'm sure you're better than she is," I said.

"I'm not," said Arielle. "She might be a prodigy. And even if she were a little worse than me, she'd still sound better with that Stradivarius."

For our school's winter concert the string orchestra would play several pieces, the band would play several pieces, and then, for the finale, the orchestra and band would join together and play a few popular songs. For the grand finale that year, the orchestra and band would play a medley from the soundtrack to *Jurassic Park*, which had been popular in theaters the past summer. Because Arielle already had her solo in the Sibelius, Olga was selected to play a duet from the *Jurassic Park* medley with Gabe Winn, who played saxophone. Each day after school Olga and Gabe would rehearse in one of the practice studios on the music hall of the school, and each afternoon Arielle would make up reasons why she needed to be in that hallway. We'd sit and listen to the music drifting out of the studio.

"A violin and sax duet is stupid," Arielle said. "It's like mixing up two completely different worlds."

I thought they sounded good together, but of course I did not say this to Arielle.

Each afternoon Arielle would linger in the music hallway, and she'd kick the wall outside the practice studio. I wondered if Olga and Gabe could hear Arielle's kicks, but if they did, they didn't stop playing.

"Let's go," I said each day, tugging on the sleeve of Arielle's puffy jacket. "Let's go home."

After about a week of this lingering I had an idea about how to distract Arielle. I'd saved up money all year from babysitting, and I was planning on using that money to buy a computer in the summer. My father told me if I could save up enough to afford half the cost of a new Macintosh, he would chip in for the other half. I decided I needed to take some of my money and buy a pair of ice skates. I'd outgrown my old ones a few years before, and my mother had replaced the laces with red ribbons and now hung them on a living room wall as part of our Christmas decorations. I would buy a new pair of skates and ask Arielle to give me lessons each afternoon. I hoped it would take her mind off Olga and Gabe.

Arielle and I went to Galaville Sporting Goods downtown, and she helped me pick out a pair of skates. She showed me how to lace them up, then held onto my arms as I stood wobbling in the skates on the carpeted floor of the store. "This will be fun," Arielle said. "After you can skate steadily, we can choreograph a number where we skate together."

The next week we headed to the pond each day after school, and Arielle patiently showed me how to skate backward, how to do a basic two-foot spin. "I don't want to jump yet," I told her, and she said we could slowly work up to jumps. I was always worried I'd hurt myself, and skating backward already seemed like a dangerous and daring thing to do.

Sometimes as we practiced there would be boys playing hockey on half the pond, skating fast, slapping a puck into a goal at one end. It was unspoken that the hockey players got the half of the pond closer to the rec center, and the skaters got the half closer to the playground. Each group tried their best to avoid the other, although the puck would often skid onto the skating half of the pond. "Sorry, sorry," the hockey players would call out as the skaters kicked the puck back onto their side. The hockey boys wore a thicker kind of skate, and they moved with manic speed, not finesse. Some days Gabe would be out on the pond with the other boys playing hockey. On those days Arielle forgot about our lessons and instead whirled around the middle of the pond, leaping and spinning, hoping Gabe would notice her, although he never did. Left on my own, I skated slowly, as far from the hockey boys as I could be, scared I'd be hit by the fast-moving puck.

"It's pretty lame to play a hockey game with only one net," Arielle said one afternoon after an hour spent trying to catch Gabe's attention. She sat on a bench next to the pond and unlaced her skates and slipped her boots back on.

There was only one net because the players needed it to practice shooting, even though they never played real games. Because half the pond was for skaters, there couldn't be two nets, except on the last day of February, when the town held its Winter Classic and a second net was hauled out from the rec center. During the Winter Classic the best players in town competed against each other, with many residents of the town circling the pond, cheering them on. After the game Anthony Lombardi, owner of Pizzeria Perfecto, would treat everyone on the winning team to free pizza. In those days the Winter Classic was something to look forward to, a bright spark in the long and dreary upstate winters.

The day after the winter concert—where Olga had played the duet with Gabe—Olga showed up at the pond. By this point her reputation had been so damaged by Arielle's lies that it was impossible for her to make female friends. I admired Olga for keeping her head down, ignoring the whispers in the hallway, and continuing to do her work. Not only was she an excellent violinist, but she was also an exemplary student, despite English being her second language. Her good grades only infuriated Arielle further.

Olga put her violin case and backpack against the base of a tree, sat down, and pulled out a pair of skates from her backpack. Instead of the white skates Arielle and I wore, she laced up a pair of black hockey skates.

"What the hell?" Arielle said. She stormed over to Olga, her own skates dangling by her side, held by the laces.

"You play hockey?" Arielle said.

Olga nodded. "My brothers taught me. These are my brother Alexi's skates. They are too small for him now."

It made sense that Olga wanted to play hockey; no girls would ever hang out with her, so why not play hockey with the boys. And now that the winter concert was over, she did not have to spend her afternoons rehearsing.

"What can't you do?" Arielle said, and Olga looked up at Arielle, but she did not respond.

"Come on," I said to Arielle. "Let's go put our skates on." As Arielle moved toward a park bench, I turned to smile at Olga. I gave her a small wave, and she waved back. It was all I could do, to wave and smile, even though I wanted to apologize profusely for the unkind and untrue rumors Arielle had been spreading about her.

Gabe was also at the park that day, and he walked toward Olga holding two hockey sticks. When he got to the tree where Olga was lacing her skates, he rested the sticks against the tree's trunk, held out his gloved hands to her, and pulled her to her feet.

"I don't feel like skating today," Arielle said.

"Please?" I said. "I think I'm ready for the single axel."

In the past week Arielle had become less patient, chastising me for being too timid, saying all great skaters had a streak of fearlessness in them. "I don't need to be a great skater," I kept telling her. "I just want to be proficient." I knew Arielle was often confused about my desire to be merely proficient—a proficient skater, a proficient bass player—when she did not want to do anything unless she could be the best. I suppose I knew I would never become a world-class skater or a professional musician, so it was enough for me to be proficient. I got good grades and knew I wanted to be a history major when I went to college. That felt like enough to be good at and to know at that point in my life.

Arielle and I sat on the bench watching the hockey game. Olga was easily able to keep pace with the boys. In fact, she was faster than all of them, and more dexterous. She weaved around them, making shot after shot. Arielle said, "She knows hockey, but she also knows figure skating. Hockey players don't skate like that."

I watched as Olga passed the puck to Gabe, and he shot it into the net. He turned around, grinned, gave her a high five.

"Let's go," Arielle said. We stood up, and I followed her, and as we walked away from the pond she bent down, picked up Olga's violin case that rested at the base of the tree, and continued to walk, Olga's violin case in one hand, the dangling ice skates in the other.

It was a beautiful violin, but it wasn't a Stradivarius. I was sure of that. We examined the violin carefully in the dim light of Arielle's basement. I refused to touch the violin, feeling a strong paranoia—spurred on by the dramas about police work I liked to watch on TV—about leaving my fingerprints on it. I crouched and looked into the F-holes and squinted, searching for the signature that appeared inside all Stradivarius violins. There was none.

"We can't keep it," I said.

"I wasn't going to," Arielle said. "That would be stupid."

"Are we going to give it back?"

"That would be stupid too."

I felt a guilty ache in my chest. Even if it wasn't a Stradivarius, the violin was likely expensive. It was made of dark polished wood and the tone was rich and warm when Arielle lifted it to her chin and drew the bow across the strings. I suspected Olga loved that violin. I wondered if her family had the money to replace it.

"Do you think Gabe is being nice to her so she'll be on his hockey team and they'll win the Winter Classic?" Arielle asked. "Did you see how good she is at hockey?"

"I don't know if Gabe really cares that much about winning. You just get a slice of free pizza if you win."

"I think everyone cares about winning," Arielle said. She ran her fingers across the top of the violin, then placed it back in its case.

"I have to go home for dinner," I said.

"It's not even four o'clock," Arielle said. "I can make you a snack here."

"We eat early in the winter. When it gets dark early."

I knew Arielle knew what I said wasn't true. She'd been over at my house for dinner plenty of times, and she knew we didn't eat until after both of my parents got home from work around six.

"Fine, go," she said.

"Please don't do anything terrible with the violin."

Arielle shrugged. "We'll see," she said as she shut the lid on the violin case and secured the latches.

After Arielle stole the violin, I pulled away from her, and this made me realize how much of my life she'd occupied. Even when we were not together I was always thinking of things to tell her, of things I needed to show her, of conversations we had to have. To fill the lonely spaces left behind after I distanced myself from Arielle, I started hanging out with other girls. I'd always been friendly with these girls but had never spent time with them outside of school. My new friends were girls who weren't popular but weren't outcasts, who were smart but not competitive, and I was surprised at how easy and uncomplicated these friendships were. We talked about TV shows and music and discussed which boys we thought were cute and made plans to go to the mall or the movies on the weekends. Once I suggested we invite Olga to join us for a movie, but the other girls shook their heads, claiming Olga was bad and their parents wouldn't want them hanging out with her. "I heard she's had three abortions," said Sally Connolly. "Can you believe it?" *No, no*, I wanted to say. I knew Olga's reputation sprang wholly from the lies Arielle had spread, but how could I defend Olga without implicating Arielle? And so I never said anything again about including Olga in our activities.

The day after her violin was stolen, Mr. Himmelman loaned Olga one of the cheap school violins in a black plastic case. Those school instruments were tinny and wretched sounding, even in the most skilled hands. They had to be easily replaceable, since they were sent home with students, and there was a good probability they'd be lost or damaged. As I played the bass and looked across the room and over the music stand Olga and Arielle shared, I wondered how Arielle could bear sitting next to Olga and listening to the sounds coming from that awful school violin.

After school that day I decided my skating days were over—skating was too closely aligned with Arielle—and donated my almost-new skates to Goodwill. That winter, I felt jealous sometimes walking home and watching the action on the pond, wishing I was part of it all, but I told myself that at least I would have less of a chance of getting injured if I just watched.

As the winter progressed, the boys practiced for longer hours for the Winter Classic. Olga was the only girl among them. She was excellent, swift and graceful, far better than the boys. I stopped each afternoon and watched the hockey games, and I finally understood why Olga bothered Arielle so much. She was good at everything, better than Arielle was, and the fact that she seemed to have little ego about her talents made her, in perhaps the most important way, better than Arielle could ever be.

In mid-February, a few weeks after Arielle stole the violin, the weather warmed. The groundhog had seen his shadow, so we knew winter wasn't over yet, but everyone was happy to shed their hats and scarves, to see some brown grass poking through the melting snow. The pond thawed into a slushy mess.

One day as I was walking home from school during the warm spell, Arielle appeared in the park. It seemed she'd darted out from behind a tree. "I miss you," Arielle said.

I was completely caught off guard. "I . . ." I said, but I could not finish by saying that I missed Arielle too. My life felt simpler, less stressful, without Arielle in it.

"My mom said you could sleep over on Friday night," Arielle said. "She said we could order pizza and she has a rent-one-get-one-free coupon from Blockbuster. I was thinking we could get *Sister Act* and *A League of Their Own*?" Arielle sounded nervous as she spoke, as if she'd memorized what she would say. We had seen those movies together in the theater the year before. Arielle knew they were my favorite movies I'd seen that year.

"Oh, thanks, but I can't," I said, and Arielle's eyes narrowed. Anger and disappointment washed over her face. I had promised some of my new friends I'd go with them to the mall on Friday. We were planning on getting second holes pierced in our ears, as long as we could convince our parents that double piercings did not mean we would become unemployable degenerates in the future.

"Yeah, whatever," Arielle said. "That's fine." And then she ran off, her backpack slapping her back as she sprinted away. I watched her run across the muddy grass. I wanted to reach my arm out and drag her back, tell her maybe we could be friends again if she could be different, if she could stop with the nastiness toward Olga. But I said nothing and just watched until she disappeared completely, leaving only a path of footprints denting the mud.

That night there was a fierce snowstorm, which blanketed our town with nine inches of snow, covering up all the footprints in the park. Overnight, the temperatures dropped precipitously, and by the next day the pond had frozen again, a thick sheet of ice and snow covering it. By morning, no traces of my meeting with Arielle remained in the park.

It was not a surprise when Olga's team won the Winter Classic, and I wondered what Arielle thought when the *Galaville Gazette* profiled Olga as its Student of the Week. I wondered how much rage and jealousy flowed through Arielle when the newspaper declared Olga to be a "scholar, athlete, and musical genius" and named Olga the MVP of the Winter Classic.

Throughout that winter, Olga played the shoddy school violin, and on many days after school she took that violin into one of the practice studios. Sometimes I could hear both Olga and Arielle playing in separate practice rooms, their music creating an awful discord. I thought about Olga's beautiful violin every day. I fantasized about breaking into Arielle's house, finding the violin, then leaving it on Olga's doorstep with no note, no clue to who had stolen it or who had returned it. But of course I did nothing beyond wondering what had happened to it and hoping Arielle had not done anything horrible.

The stretch of days after the Winter Classic and before the weather warmed always felt so long, so dull and gray, but that year Chuckie Dutton saved a four-year-old girl from drowning during the second week of March and that caused excitement that lasted for weeks. Chuckie was a junior, and he wanted to go to Union, where he hoped to play hockey, to move beyond that one-net pond in Sutter's Park. Because our town had no rink and no hockey team, he hoped to somehow prove himself to college recruiters. A week after most of the other hockey players had put away their skates for the season, Chuckie continued to go to the pond to practice wrist shots. One afternoon he arrived at the park and was prepared to do a tentative test of the solidity of the ice when he saw a small hand waving from a hole in the middle of the pond. He dropped his skates and stick and ran onto the pond. The pond felt like it would give way under his feet, and the cracking ice sounded like a frantically ticking clock. Chuckie lowered himself to his belly, slid on the ice until he was right next to the hole, reached in, but could not find anything to grasp onto. The pond wasn't terribly deep—about six feet at its deepest—but the hand he'd seen was small and the pond was deep enough to swallow a child. In that moment there was only one thing Chuckie could do: plunge into the hole, submerge himself, and see if he could find the child. So he sat up, slid into the icy water feet first, dropped down and opened his eyes and saw a dark pink coat and blonde hair and looped his arm around a little girl. Then he saw something else, and with his other hand he reached for it, then he shot up out of the water, a cold, gasping girl in one arm, and a waterlogged, ice-covered violin in the other.

I knew the details of the rescue from the town newspaper and because everyone at school couldn't stop talking about Chuckie's pond rescue. We even had an assembly where the Fire Department came and presented Chuckie with an award for bravery, and the entire auditorium exploded with cheers as Chuckie accepted it. The drowning girl was Natalie Buckhaven, who lived on Maple Street. She had slipped out the back door of her house and wandered off to the park while her mother thought she was taking a nap and had glided onto the pond, pretending to be Kristi Yamaguchi skating at the Olympics. Both she and Chuckie were fine after a few hours at the hospital, where they were warmed up and given fluids. The violin, I was certain, was Olga's. There had been a rope tied to the neck of the violin, and Chuckie swore he'd seen a brick attached to the other end of the rope, but the rope had loosened on his way up out of the pond. "What a super weird thing to find in the pond!" he was quoted as saying in the newspaper. Olga said nothing about any of it. I don't know what happened to the violin Chuckie pulled up, but I assumed it was a useless mass of wet wood that could not be repaired. I was certain Arielle had submerged the violin on the last night the pond was melted, on the night I turned down her offer to sleep over at her house. I told myself that maybe if I'd accepted Arielle's offer, then I could have convinced Arielle to return the violin. And so I felt complicit, even though I had never once touched that violin.

In the fall, Olga was gone. Mr. Himmelman told us Olga had been accepted at a prestigious performing arts school halfway across the country, in Michigan. "We'll certainly miss her," he said, sorrow in his voice. I looked at Arielle, who was once again in the concert-mistress's spot. She refused to meet my eyes. She played an A, and the rest of the orchestra was supposed to tune their instruments to her note. That day, Olga gone, Arielle back in the first chair, I turned my tuning pegs until my bass was completely out of tune. Back then it felt like something significant I was doing, a way of damaging the orchestra and not following Arielle's lead. But now, of course, I know it was a silly, useless gesture. It would be an understatement to say that it was not enough, that all my actions back then were not enough. I had not stolen or even touched Olga's violin. I had not drowned it in the pond. I had not spread rumors about Olga. But, still, I was complicit in my quiet, scared way. Now, when I look back on my early years, it's not what I did that I regret, but rather how much I did not do.

MRS. WHITSON'S FACE

Something is very different about your guidance counselor's face when you return to school in September. She looks like a Muppet, not one of the colorful furry ones, but one of the weird human ones with features that are off-kilter. During lunch on the first day of school your friends speculate about what happened over the summer: maybe she'd gotten into a car accident and had to have plastic surgery to put her face back together. Maybe she'd been in a fire and new skin was still growing over where the old skin had been. Maybe this wasn't really Mrs. Whitson but a look-alike who only kind of resembled her. Maybe, maybe, maybe.

After listening to them go on and on, you say, "You guys are so dumb. She got Botox and fillers." You've watched enough reality TV featuring nipped and tucked D-list celebrities to know what the results of these procedures look like.

Nicole, Michiko, and Alexis all stop talking and stare at you.

"Why, though?" Nicole finally says.

"Why not?" you say. "Who knows why people do stupid things?"

"Isn't Botox for rich people?" Alexis asks.

You understand why they're asking these questions. In your little upstate town, you don't see people with their skin pulled tight. When people get old, they allow wrinkles to set in, let their jowls sag, sigh about the loose skin on their necks but don't do anything about it. There are better things to spend money on.

You laugh. "It's not like she got a facelift. I think a guidance counselor can afford Botox." You wonder if there's actually a doctor in this town who does these cosmetic procedures, or whether Mrs. Whitson had to travel far to get needles stuck in her face.

"Her eyebrows," says Michiko. "They're, like, frozen. She looks surprised."

"Bad work," you say. You try to project confidence, but you're not certain if it's really bad work or if this is how her face is supposed to look. After all, many celebrities have the same weird surprised expression and strange over-plumped cheeks, and sometimes they even have disturbing duck lips. These are people who have enough money to go to the best plastic surgeons and dermatologists.

But in your group it's your job to know things, so you repeat: "It's so obviously bad work." You lived in Manhattan until you were six, when your father lost his job in finance and your family moved upstate for a simpler—which you now understand to mean cheaper—life in your mother's hometown. It's not that your friends are rubes, exactly, but they've never lived anywhere but Galaville. They need you to teach them about the world; this is what you have to offer your little group of friends.

Your friends are smarter than you are. Everyone knows this, but it's never been said out loud. But now it's your senior year and you'll all be applying to colleges soon, and then it will be obvious who is smart and who is not. Not only is Michiko smart, but she's the captain of the soccer team and is good enough to play for the U.S. women's national team one day. Her coach told her that. Nicole wants to be a doctor, has known it since she was a little girl and her sister had leukemia and doctors saved her life. She acts like biology is the most interesting thing in the world. You make fun of her for being a nerd, but secretly you think that if you were ever diagnosed with a horrible disease, Nicole would be the only person you'd trust to take care of you. Alexis is a poet and has won prizes both for spoken word and for her poems that are written out. You like her spoken word stuff better; the way she performs—happy or sad or angry—helps you understand what the poems mean. Alexis won a scholarship to a summer writers workshop last year; she beat out seven hundred other kids for the scholarship. And of course she's good at everything else, smart about classes that involve reading and writing and smart, too, about classes that involve numbers. And you? You are good at art. But where is that going to get you in the world? No one in your high school cares about art. They care about sports and academics. Art is an afterthought, which is obvious to anyone who's ever looked at the art classroom, which is the old teacher's lounge converted into an art classroom by bringing in four long plastic folding tables.

In October you each have to meet with Mrs. Whitson, who will help you come up with a list of colleges you should apply to. Your friends have their appointments before you do; the appointments are scheduled alphabetically by last name, and since your last name begins with Y, you are one of the last to go. At lunch, your friends compare their lists. You see Ivy League schools on each of their lists. You see schools in places you'd want to live: big, bright, exciting cities. You dread your appointment with Mrs. Whitson.

On October 16th you have an appointment with her at 1:15, so you get to leave English class early, which is an enormous relief. You have read *Jane Eyre* but you don't understand it. You've read the words—every single one in the book—but they don't come together to form something that makes sense. You get distracted, your mind zigging and zagging. You know you should ask Alexis to help you figure it out, but you're embarrassed to ask. Why doesn't your mind do the zigging and zagging when you read magazines or websites about celebrities? Maybe it's the photos; maybe images help keep you focused.

When you sit down across from Mrs. Whitson you think she is smiling at you, but you're not sure. Her face is still strange, although whatever was shot into it seems to have loosened its grip a little since the beginning of the school year.

"Maya," she says, "how's senior year going for you?"

You shrug. It's going. What does she want to know? Does she want to know that you're scared that soon this year will be over and your friends will all move away and none of them will stay in touch? Does she want to know that you're worried they're all still friends with you only out of habit? Does she want to know that you're aware they're all smarter and nicer than you are, and you don't feel like you really belong with them nowadays? After you moved upstate, your four families pitched in for after-school care, and a woman whom you loved—Beatrice—watched over all four kids on weekdays between the hours when you got home from school and when your parents got home from work. Once a week, Beatrice would come up with an art project for the four of you to work on. The other girls were entertained enough by these art projects, but you became obsessed with them, working and working for days on a project that was only supposed to take a few hours.

"How's your art class going?" says Mrs. Whitson. "You'll be part of the senior show next month, right?"

You nod. You are doing charcoal portraits of your three best friends for the show. You want to capture them just as they are right now, so you will have these drawings to look at when they are far away. You know the generous thing to do would be to give each friend her portrait, but you want to keep them for yourself. You'll take photos of each of them standing next to her portrait during the senior show, and you will print out and frame these photos, and that will be enough to give away.

"And what will your contribution be?"

"Portraits," you say.

"Self-portraits?"

"No." You shake your head. You hate self-portraits, would never want to spend hours and hours staring at your own image in a mirror in order to draw yourself. "Portraits of Michiko, Alexis, and Nicole."

"That sounds lovely," says Mrs. Whitson. "You four are such good friends."

You stare hard at her face. You can't tell if she really thinks it's lovely or not. Her expression hasn't changed at all. And now you think about whether you can get Botox right before graduation. Are seventeen-year-olds allowed to get Botox? Wouldn't it be nice to freeze your face so no one can tell from your expression what you're thinking?

"It's wonderful how the four of you have always been there for each other," Mrs. Whitson says.

You nod, but you don't say anything. You don't want to be tricked into talking about feelings. You've heard Mrs. Whitson has degrees in social work and psychology. Sometimes people go talk to her about their problems, even if they're not academic problems. You're not a hundred percent sure what sort of counseling a guidance counselor is supposed to offer, but Alexis went to see Mrs. Whiston once a week for an entire semester when her parents were going through a divorce. She said Mrs. Whitson was helpful and a good listener, but you laughed and said that if she really was qualified to be an actual therapist, why would she be in a stuffy, windowless office in a high school?

"I suppose we should get down to business," says Mrs. Whitson. "I came up with a list of schools I think would be good fits for you." She spins in her chair and reaches for a sheet of paper sitting on top of her printer. "Take a look," she says.

You glance down at the list. There are two nearby community colleges on it and then some SUNY schools, one so far away it's almost in Canada. It's a very different list from your friends' lists.

"I was thinking Yale," you say, looking up from the list. "Or Princeton." You know these schools are impossibilities for you, but you want to see if you can get Mrs. Whitson's face to move. It doesn't budge. She just picks up her coffee mug and takes a long swig.

"The list is just a suggestion," she says when she's finished drinking. "I looked to see if there were schools with good art programs. And don't write off community college. You could do an associate's degree in art and then think about what the next step is."

There are no private schools on the list, and you wonder whether she thinks your family can't afford it. You don't know if they can or can't. Your family has a nice enough house and two cars and you've certainly never gone hungry. Your parents own a store that sells little gifts, like candles that smell like desserts and goat's milk soaps and clay mugs made by local potters. Your father often declares that he likes this life much better than the life he led working in finance in Manhattan. But how many soaps would he have to sell to send you to a private college? The town is small enough that Mrs. Whitson likely knows that your parents sell gifts and trinkets. Maybe this is part of the reason she's suggesting community college. Is it possible that your family is actually struggling financially and you just don't know it?

"I might not go to college," you say. You're not sure if this is true or not, but you are mad about the list of colleges Mrs. Whitson gave you. You pick up the list, crumple it, and Mrs. Whitson looks down at her desk. Now you have the balled-up list in your hand, and you don't know what to do with it.

"That's your decision, but I'm here to help you in any way I can. Did you sign up for tutoring, like we talked about last year?"

You squeeze the crumpled paper hard in your hand. "I don't need tutoring," you say. The tutors are all annoying overachievers who only volunteer because they want to be involved in a million activities so colleges will think they are interesting people who are generous with their time. The tutoring is free and after school in the high school library, and if anyone goes into the library it's so obvious what's happening. The best students in the school and the worst students in the school—people who would never normally be seen together—are hunched over books at the same tables. It might have been one thing to be tutored as a freshman, but there's no way you're getting tutored now as a senior by another senior.

"Well, it doesn't seem like you need anything, Maya, so you're free to go." Mrs. Whitson stands up.

You are surprised by the suddenness of this. You thought you'd go back and forth for longer. But then you realize you're probably not worth her time. Why waste time on you when she's got kids bound for the Ivy League who actually want to come and talk to her, who want to tell her their problems and listen to her solutions?

You don't stand up. You squeeze the balled-up paper in your hand again, and you stare at her face, at her too-plump cheeks that have definitely been injected with something. You stare at her forehead and the corners of her eyes, where there used to be wrinkles. You stare so hard and then you see something red.

"Are you okay?" Mrs. Whitson says.

"Your face is bleeding," you say. What you see is a bunch of red spots swimming before your eyes. They aren't just on Mrs. Whitson's face; they are all over the room, zigging and zagging, like your brain when you try to read.

"My what?" she says, raising a hand to her face.

"No," you say, shaking your head. You blink hard, twice, and when you open your eyes again the spots are gone. "I just saw a red spot. Or a few. Like in my eye. Your face, it's fine."

You're not sure what to wear on the night of the art show. You haven't ever met a real artist in your life, so you don't know how they dress. Mr. Paulson, your art teacher, always wears a tucked-in white button-down shirt and khakis and brown leather shoes and a black leather belt that does not match the brown shoes. He carries a tan leather briefcase and wears large, gold-rimmed glasses that Alexis calls serial killer glasses, insisting that every serial killer wears the same ones. If you didn't know he was an art teacher you would guess he was an accountant or a bank teller. You're not sure how he ever became an art teacher. He doesn't seem to even like art.

You think artists usually wear black, so you dig around in your closet and find a black dress that you wore a few years ago to the funeral of a granduncle you'd never met. The sleeves are puffy and there's a line of pearly buttons down the front and it looks like a dress for a little girl, but it's the best you can do. You put on black tights and a pair of black rubber gardening clogs. The clogs are probably a little funny, but it's fine. You're an artist and artists can wear whatever they want and people will just say they are being artistic.

Your parents are more excited about the art show than they should be. They've dressed up for the occasion, even though you think no other parents will be dressed up. They've already seen the portraits, have watched as they developed over the course of a few weeks. "There's nothing new to see tonight," you tell them, but they insist on coming.

"Don't you look nice," says your father as you walk into the kitchen.

"You're only saying that because I'm wearing a dress," you say.

"Are those my gardening clogs?" says your mother. You'd forgotten you'd borrowed them from her and didn't give them back. "I've been looking all over for them."

"Oh, yeah," you say.

"Do you want to borrow some nicer shoes?"

You shrug. "These are fine," you say and you're glad when she doesn't argue.

The three of you get in the car and your mother hums the entire way to school. Your parents are acting like they're going somewhere exciting, even though they are only going to the high school to look at artwork taped up to the cafeteria walls. But maybe this is about as exciting as their lives get in Galaville. Maybe this is the biggest and most thrilling thing they've done all year.

Michiko, Alexis, and Nicole are already in the cafeteria when you arrive. The long brown tables have been pushed to one side of the room, the benches attached to the tables folded up on top of them. There is a group of boys standing near your friends, laughing with them. "You should look at everyone else's stuff," you say to your parents. "You've already seen mine." You hope they take the hint and disappear.

Michiko waves you over. She is standing in front of her portrait. In the portrait she is wearing her goalkeeper's gloves and holding a soccer ball in front of her chest. She looks determined and fierce in the portrait, bright natural light illuminating the right half of her face. In real life she is wearing a dress with daisies on it and lipstick whose color you know is called Bubblegum Fun. Matty Drexler looks at her portrait and says, "I would be scared if I saw this version of Michiko walking down the street."

"You should be scared of me *all* the time," Michiko says. "Especially on the soccer field." She gives him that intense look that's on her face in her portrait. Matty laughs. He's on the boys' soccer team and is good enough that he'll probably get a scholarship to play in college. The thing is, he's not as good as Michiko, but because he's a boy he gets taken more seriously as an athlete. Michiko works harder than he does, trains more than he does, but she knows that even as good as she is, she won't get into a top college without excellent grades backing up her athletic skills. Michiko knows Matty likes her, but she won't let anything happen between them because she can't handle how easy it is for him as an athlete, how he never has to prove himself, how everyone just automatically respects him. She knows that if they spend time together, her resentment of him—and all the semi-decent male athletes at the high school—will only expand until it explodes.

"You did this?" says Matty, pointing to Michiko's portrait.

You nod.

"Can I, like, buy it from you?"

"Oh my god," Michiko says. "Don't be creepy."

Alexis and Nicole laugh.

"You don't have enough money," you say.

"Name your price," says Matty.

"Two million," says Alexis. "I'm her agent."

"One point five," says Matty.

"One point seven."

"One point six."

"Deal," says Alexis, and she reaches out to shake Matty's hand. He laughs loudly, but you know it wasn't a joke, that he wanted the portrait of Michiko. Maybe he would have been willing to give you forty or fifty dollars for it. But you won't let anyone buy these portraits. They are yours.

"I'm off to withdraw my millions from the bank," Matty says, and he and his friends move away from your artwork toward some watercolors displayed near the garbage can.

Now it's just the four of you standing in front of your portraits. Alexis and Nicole tell you they love their portraits. "You're amazing," says Alexis, but you shrug it off. She is prone to exaggeration. This afternoon she called the peaches in syrup that were served in the cafeteria "amazing" too.

All three of the portraits feature dramatic light and shadows, a technique you learned by studying Caravaggio's paintings. You suddenly wish Mrs. Whitson were here. You'd tell her about Caravaggio and ask if she knows who he was. You'd tell her you are not stupid and you would offer to be an art tutor. But of course there's no such thing. Art is not considered something people need to do well in in order to succeed at your high school.

You're able to block out the chatter in the cafeteria for a moment and stare at the three portraits on the wall. You see something red beneath them, and worry for a second that the red spots in your eyes are back, but it's just a stain on the wall, probably from ketchup. You debated making a background or frame to attach the three portraits to in order to make a triptych, but then you decided against it. You'd be linking your three friends without including yourself, and that would be like announcing you are not part of their group. And you are part of it, at least for now.

You take a step back and try to look at the portraits objectively. You know you are better at drawing than everyone else in your school, but it isn't enough. You can manage not to flinch when you get a math test back with a D on it, but you want to scream when you notice that Nicole's eyes are just a tiny bit too close together in your portrait. And now that you can study the three portraits on the wall in the bad cafeteria lighting, you think there's something immature and awful about them. Michiko is holding her soccer ball, Nicole has a stethoscope around her neck, and Alexis is standing behind a microphone, looking as if she's about to begin a spoken word poem. The props were a stupid idea. These portraits look like something people could get at Disneyland, quick sketches made by a park employee who asks, "What's your favorite activity?" and then draws a cartoon of the person doing that activity. You want to rip these portraits off the wall and start again. You are furious.

"Hey," says Nicole, "hey! Are you okay?"

"What?" you say, looking away from the portrait. You look at real-life Nicole with her eyes spaced the correct distance apart and you want to cry.

"You just looked like you went to another planet for a second," Nicole says.

"I screwed up your eyes."

Nicole looks at the portrait then shrugs. "I love it. It's perfect."

No, it's not perfect. How can Nicole—who is all about precise measurements and getting the formulas and equations right in math and science classes—just give you a pass for eyes that are too close together? It is not exact, it is not right, and it bothers you so, so much. You are good at one thing and one thing only, and you hate when you mess up.

"Maya," Nicole says, putting her hand on your arm, "I'm not kidding. These are so good." She leans in close to you and whispers, "They're so obviously better than everyone else's."

"Your eyes, though," you say.

"If you wanted to get everything exactly perfect, you could have just taken a picture. Stuff like the eyes not being perfect is what makes the portrait feel, I don't know, human."

Human, you think. Human is good, right?

"Maya," you hear a voice call from behind you. You turn and see your parents and Mrs. Whitson and Beatrice, your babysitter from years ago. They are all walking toward you, and this feels like something out of a strange dream where people from different parts of your life have all come together, even though they'd never be together in real life. You haven't seen Beatrice in years, not since you were twelve. What is she doing here? She looks very old, more stooped and wrinkled than you remember, and you wonder why you hadn't noticed how old she was when she used to babysit you. Mrs. Whitson's hand is gripping Beatrice's upper arm, steadying her as she walks. Why is Mrs. Whitson touching your babysitter?

"Look who we ran into," says your mother, smiling widely.

"My goodness," says Beatrice, waving a hand toward Alexis, Michiko, and Nicole. "My girls, all of them still together."

Alexis flings herself toward Beatrice, hugs her hard and you, Michiko, and Nicole exchange looks. Alexis can do these sorts of things—she's a poet and overly emotional behavior is acceptable for poets—but the rest of you don't know what to do.

"Girls," says Beatrice, "how good to see you all. And Maya, this is your artwork? I knew when you were just a little girl that you would be an artist."

"Really?" you say, but you don't know if she's being honest with you. This seems like the kind of thing adults say mindlessly to young people in order to make them feel good.

"Do you want to take a closer look at the portraits, Aunt Beatrice?" says Mrs. Whitson.

You and your friends exchange quick looks.

Aunt Beatrice? Nicole mouths.

Whaaaaaat? mouths Alexis.

"You're related?" you ask. No one else is going to do it, so you might as well.

"Yes, Ally is my niece," says Beatrice. "She brought me tonight, insisted it would be good for me to get out of the house."

"Did you know she used to babysit us?" Michiko asks, and Mrs. Whitson shakes her head.

"I knew she used to babysit a group of girls, but somehow I never put together that it was the four of you," Mrs. Whitson says. "Sometimes I forget how small this town is."

Beatrice says, "Maya, can you believe that once upon a time Ally was a very good artist, too?"

"Oh, not really," Mrs. Whitson immediately jumps in to say.

You feel dizzy; it's so strange that Beatrice is calling Mrs. Whitson by her first name.

"I seem to remember that big fight with your parents about your college major," says Beatrice, and all four of you—you, Michiko, Nicole, and Alexis—stare greedily at Beatrice, waiting for her to say more.

"Well, they won, didn't they? They said psychology was more practical than fine arts, and I suppose they were right," Mrs. Whitson says. "I never took an art class again after high school." Her voice sounds strained, like someone has just punched her stomach. Then she looks at you, and something in her seems to shift, and she's back to the guidance counselor, not the niece, when she says, "But of course just because an art major wasn't right for me, it doesn't mean it isn't right for everyone." And then there's a softening again, something human, as Nicole would say, appearing, and she adds, "And anyway, I was nowhere near as talented as Maya."

For a moment you can imagine her as a little girl named Ally who liked to draw. Then you think of her as a teenager fighting with her parents about her major. You feel a squeeze of discomfort in your gut as you realize Mrs. Whitson has a whole life outside that windowless office, that she hasn't always been the person who hands over lists of possible college choices to ungrateful students.

You look at your parents, who are standing there in their dress-up clothes, as if they are attending some fancy gallery opening and not in the high school cafeteria looking at drawings taped to the dirty walls. They are beaming, their pride evident on their faces. No one has ever called you talented in front of them. People have called you distracted and not living up to your potential and a space cadet and in need of tutoring.

Beatrice waves her hand. "Talent is overrated. It's hard work that's made Maya so good. Even as a little girl she worked and worked on her drawings. I couldn't believe someone so young could concentrate for so long."

Your parents continue to beam, and you wish they would say something instead of just standing there like grinning zombies. You wish they would say that you actually work hard at a lot of things, even though your grades don't reflect this hard work.

"Well, let's get a closer look," Beatrice says, and Mrs. Whitson's hand goes back to Beatrice's upper arm, but Beatrice shakes her off. "I can manage," she says, but when she walks she's a little shaky.

Beatrice examines all three portraits closely, pauses for a long time before each one, as if she's looking at Van Goghs in a museum. "Chiaroscuro," she says, then turns to Mrs. Whitson and says, "do you know that term?"

Mrs. Whitson shakes her head and once again she looks like a little girl, not like someone who knows the answers. How is it possible that someone with a Botoxed face can suddenly look like a child?

"Anyone?" says Beatrice, and your friends—your Ivy League–bound friends—all shake their heads. Your parents stay silent too.

"Of course you know, Maya," says Beatrice, and you nod.

"Maybe one day you can draw my portrait," says Beatrice. "But I get to choose the lighting. No harsh lighting for me, no sunlight directly on these wrinkles." She laughs, and everyone else does too, even though it's not really funny.

"These faces," says Mrs. Whitson, taking a step closer to look at the three portraits. You wait for Mrs. Whitson to finish her sentence, but she doesn't, she just stares and stares.

Then Beatrice says, "I bet you still think of yourself as looking like this. I know I do."

Mrs. Whitson still doesn't say anything, just continues to stare at your drawings.

"Girls," says Beatrice, "save these portraits. One day you'll be as old as I am, and you might still feel young on the inside but you won't look like it on the outside."

You glance at your mother, who is nodding. You wonder how old she feels on the inside. You think about the photographs you've seen of her in high school—at *this* high school—the ones from the cheerleading team, which you've laughed relentlessly about. You wonder if she thinks about those cheerleading days when she is restocking the goat's milk soaps or dusting the wind chimes in the store. Back when she was a cheerleader, who did she think she'd grow up to be?

You can't imagine being as old as Beatrice or even as old as Mrs. Whitson. You can only imagine yourself looking exactly like you do right now, but you know that will change. You wonder if Mrs. Whitson got Botox so she could look in the mirror and pretend to be someone younger, maybe someone who still has possibilities ahead of her, not someone who has to come to a small, windowless office and listen to other people's troubles and try to solve problems that are often unsolvable.

"Should we look at the rest of the artwork?" says Mrs. Whitson, stepping back from your portraits. Beatrice nods. You see Mrs. Whitson looking at Beatrice, her hand up near her own waist, trying to figure out if she should offer Beatrice her arm.

"I'm so glad I got to see all of you girls tonight," Beatrice says. "What a treat to see you've all turned out to be such wonderful young ladies. And you, Maya, your art is terrific."

You each hug Beatrice, and you wait a minute while your parents catch up with her. You hear both your mom and your dad talk about how proud they are of you, and you hear Beatrice say she's not surprised at all you turned out to be such a wonderful artist. You pretend you don't hear any of it.

After Mrs. Whitson and Beatrice go off to look at the other artwork, your parents say they will head home as long as you can catch a ride with someone else. Alexis says she'll drive you home. Your parents leave and now there's no one looking at your portraits anymore, so you line up each of your friends in front of her portrait and take photos on your phone. And then you stand in a circle and you text each of them their picture.

"I feel sort of like a celebrity," Michiko says. "Like when else in my life is someone going to draw me?"

"I'm making this my profile picture," says Alexis.

"Me too," says Nicole.

"You can each have your portrait," you say, surprising yourself. "Once the art show is over, I'll take them off the wall and roll them up and give them to you. They've already been sprayed with fixative." This way, not only will they each remember who they once were when they were seventeen, but they will remember you too. If they bring these portraits to college, they will literally have your fingerprints, dark charcoal swirls, on their walls. They will not forget you, they will not forget this night when you were called talented and hard-working, and this is how you want them to remember you, even far in the future, even when one day they are a busy doctor and the captain of the U.S. women's soccer team and a prize-winning poet and you are working some dull job in a dark and sad office. Even if all those years in the future you are doing something far from artistic in order to earn a steady paycheck, you want them to remember this one night when other people said you were full of so much potential.

MIGRATION

Vanessa's mother's house is a disaster. There are newspapers—not even real papers, but *Pennysavers*—piled in the living room, some of them from years ago. "They're for lining the birdcages," her mother insists, but the birds are not *in* the cages and Vanessa suspects they are never in the cages, which are piled one on top of another, lining an entire wall of the living room. The birds are flying free, squawking, leaving gloopy white messes everywhere. The noise is unbearable, the trills and screeches and chirps, and Vanessa wonders how her mother is able to think with this noise. How many birds are there? Thirty? Forty? Fifty? It feels as if there are a thousand, swooping overhead, landing violently on the mantle, bopping across the dining room table, a small gray one settling on Vanessa's shoulder. The bird is impervious to Vanessa's flicking, its tiny, disgusting feet digging deep into her leather jacket. Vanessa peers into the kitchen and sees decades worth of empty Cool Whip containers, which her mother says are for storing leftovers, but when was the last time her mother cooked anything in the filthy kitchen? "Do you have any wine?" Vanessa asks. There must be a glass somewhere in this mess that she can scrub clean before pouring wine into it.

"No, no wine, Nessie," Constance says. "I maybe have a bottle of grape juice in the pantry. Want me to go look for it?" Her daughter shakes her head. Constance notes her daughter's sourpuss face. She sees Nessie surveying her home. Always, even as a little girl, Nessie thought of herself as better than Constance and better than the twins, Jilly and Jules. Nessie and her father had an affinity for each other, but Stanley hasn't been in the picture for twenty years. Constance has no idea if Nessie and Stanley still stay in touch. Stanley lives in Vegas with his second wife, a woman who is supposedly a realtor, but based on the photographs on their yearly Christmas cards she could be a very successful Dolly Parton impersonator. Nessie lives in New York City, has a fancy job as a television producer, and thinks she's better than the rest of the family because they still live in Albany. Constance knows Nessie thinks they are living boring and provincial lives upstate. She knows Nessie looks down on her for her job as a cashier at Walgreens. She knows Nessie looks down on her sisters for never leaving their hometown, for going to college at a school ten minutes from their home and then finding jobs nearby. And now Nessie has returned, and Constance is suspicious of what she wants. She called yesterday, said she was coming for a visit, wanted to talk about something. Constance offered to clean out Nessie's old bedroom, but Nessie said, "I've already booked a hotel." Constance was relieved. It would take weeks to clean out Nessie's old room, to shovel through the books and clothing and bags and bags of birdseed.

"Can we go somewhere?" Vanessa says. She wants to get out of this mess. It smells like sour milk and rotten fruit. "Let me buy you dinner."

"We can't leave. The twins are coming. They're going to pick up something from Boston Market."

Vanessa can't eat surrounded by this squalor. She'd hoped to avoid her sisters, but of course her mother has summoned the troops. Jilly and Jules are adult women who are still hanging onto their childhood nicknames. Jillian and Julianne are perfectly fine names, but at thirty-eight her sisters still refuse to shed the nicknames. She switched from Nessie to Vanessa when she left home for Barnard. She knew at eighteen that she didn't want to share a nickname with a mythical Scottish lake creature. Her sisters will soon be clattering around the house, urging her to eat rotisserie chicken off plastic plates, and it will be harder for her to ask her mother to be the subject of an upcoming crossover episode of *Quick Fix* and *Animal Collectors* in their presence. "Collectors" is a kind word Vanessa and the other producers came up with to describe what the people they profile do. "Collections" summons images of china figurines or stamps, not the squalid houses the people with too many animals live in. *Quick Fix* is exactly what it sounds like: carpenters and electricians and plumbers and interior decorators march into a rundown house and fix it up in a week.

Vanessa proposed this crossover show at a meeting during which her boss told her 40 percent of the producers at the network would be losing their jobs. Vanessa can't lose her job; her job is the most important thing in her life. The crossover, *Quick Fix Animal Collector*, was the only idea to spring immediately into her mind: find someone with a crumbling house filled with animal filth, clean it out and fix it up, all in two weeks. *Quick Fix* and *Animal Collectors* were the two most popular shows on the network, so maybe a crossover would bring in an unprecedented number of viewers. When her boss asked if she had subjects lined up for the show, Vanessa lied and said her mother agreed to be the subject of the first episode. She wished she had another idea, one that didn't involve anyone from her family, but she had to hurry and get at least one episode filmed in order for the network to consider it for the fall lineup. There was no time to go out and search for subjects. She didn't want anyone from work inside her mother's home, judging it. She didn't want her mother's filthy house broadcast on national television. She didn't want anyone to know this was what she came from. But she'd said it, and her boss greeted the idea with enthusiasm, said maybe the show could feature an interview with Vanessa talking about what it was like to be a hoarder's daughter.

Now she thinks if the show is what will save her job, then it will be worth spilling her family's secrets on television.

The doorbell rings, and Constance is grateful her other daughters have arrived. Jilly and Jules can help her deal with whatever it is Nessie wants. Huey, the gray budgie on Nessie's shoulder, takes flight, heads toward the door. Huey is a dumb one; he doesn't know when people don't like him, doesn't know when he should make himself scarce. She should have never bought him in the first place. She likes brightly colored birds—they cheer up her house and make her feel good when she's in a bad mood—but the day she went to the pet store after a particularly unpleasant interaction with a customer at Walgreens, Huey was the only small bird they had, and she was not about to leave without a new bird. Constance opens the door and it is not Jilly and Jules standing there, but of course it wouldn't be. They don't ring the doorbell. They come right in because they are comfortable here, not strangers like Vanessa has become. It is Zephyr Duncan, the daughter of the hippies next door. She is wearing her Girl Scouts uniform and carrying a clipboard. Huey swoops down from Nessie's shoulder and lands on Zephyr's clipboard.

"He won't hurt you," Constance says. And now there are two people in her home who want something from her. Zephyr has obviously come to hawk cookies, and Constance still doesn't know what her daughter wants. "Let me get my wallet," Constance says, and Zephyr asks if she wants to hear about this year's new cookies. Constance waves her hand, tells her she'll get a few boxes of the chocolaty minty ones as she climbs the stairs. "Thin Mints," says Zephyr, and Constance says yes, even though she's pretty sure there are still a few boxes left in the pantry from last year.

Vanessa can hear her mother stomping around upstairs, sorting through whatever it is that's up there, looking for her wallet. The girl stands on the front porch, and Vanessa is unsure whether to invite her in or not, so she doesn't. Instead, she points to the gray bird that is still standing on the clipboard and says, "I should thank you for getting that bird off my shoulder."

The girl says, "Do you like birds?" and Vanessa says, "I'm more of a dog person."

Zephyr nods. This woman looks a little like Jilly and Jules, but she is skinny and fashionable and nervous-looking, and Jilly and Jules are none of these things. This woman is wearing a black leather jacket and tight dark jeans and high heels and is holding a large leather bag that looks stuffed and heavy. Zephyr examines the mess in the living room and realizes there's nowhere for this woman to set down the bag.

"Are you Jilly and Jules's sister?" Zephyr asks. She lifts the clipboard and shakes it a bit, but the bird just adjusts itself, climbs higher up the clipboard and settles on the silver clip.

"I am. I'm Vanessa." She extends a hand for a shake, but Zephyr cannot let go of the clipboard with the bird on it, so Vanessa just waves her inside. Zephyr has never been inside before. Her family talks to Constance on the sidewalk or in the driveway or they wave at each other from their backyards. The inside of the house has an old garbage smell.

"I'm Zephyr. I live next door."

"Oh, the Griffin house. Or I guess not anymore. Unless you're related to the Griffins?"

Zephyr shakes her head. "My last name is Duncan. My family moved here two years ago from Utica."

Vanessa can still hear her mother clomping around upstairs. Is this what it's like every time she goes out? Does she always need to budget extra time for finding her wallet? She makes a mental note to ask her friend Grant, the carpenter from *Quick Fix*, to build a little nook near the front door where her mother can keep her keys and wallet.

Vanessa says, "How much are the cookies?"

"Five dollars a box."

Vanessa slips a hand into her bag, pulls out a wallet that looks like it's made from the skin of a snake, and takes out a twenty-dollar bill. "Put my mom down for four boxes, okay?"

Zephyr nods and stares at the money Vanessa is holding out to her. She is not sure how to reach for the bill without letting go of the clipboard, and if she lets go of the clipboard, the bird will fall. But maybe it won't; birds can fly.

"Oh, here," says Vanessa, and she takes the clipboard from Zephyr, holds it straight out with one arm, gives Zephyr the twenty-dollar bill with her other hand. "Shoo," Vanessa says, waving the clipboard up and down and finally the gray bird flies off the clipboard and right back onto Vanessa's shoulder. "This bird," says Vanessa, "this one is my least favorite of them all." She hands the clipboard back to Zephyr.

Zephyr writes down the order for four boxes of Thin Mints. "I'll deliver them when they come in," she says and heads out the door. Vanessa is flicking the bird on her shoulder and seems not to have heard her. Constance still hasn't returned, and Zephyr needs to go to the other houses on their street. But she knows no matter how hard she tries she won't sell as many cookies as the other girls because other people's parents take the order forms to work and everyone at work buys cookies and her parents can't do that because they both work from home. And so she will never win the good prizes, like a kayaking trip or a vacation to Disneyland, or even the okay prizes, like a sleeping bag or a camping lantern.

"Zephyr?" says Vanessa, when the girl is halfway down the steps. "Can you hear the birds from your house?" Vanessa's ears are ringing and her head is pounding. How can her mother do anything in peace—watch TV, talk on the phone, eat dinner—with all these bird noises?

Zephyr's face blanches. "Why?" she asks.

"I was just curious."

Zephyr can certainly hear the birds. They squawk all the time. Mostly they make ugly sounds, but sometimes they chirp, and once in a while there is a beautiful song that Zephyr can hear drifting into her bedroom window. But her parents won't complain because a year ago Zephyr's mother built a chicken coop and they have a dozen chickens and one rooster that crows every morning at 5:00 a.m. and the other neighbors have complained, but Constance has not. The other neighbors wrote a letter to the police citing the Duncans for noise pollution, but Constance would not sign it because she claimed that never, not once, had she been woken up by the rooster, and the police said if the next-door neighbor couldn't hear the rooster, then it couldn't be that loud. And so Zephyr and her family pretend they cannot hear the birds and every Sunday Zephyr's oldest brother, Sage, fills a basket with freshly laid eggs and leaves it on Constance's stoop.

"I can't really hear them. I guess they don't chirp that loudly," Zephyr says.

"Right," says Vanessa, although it's clear the girl is lying. "Well, good luck with the cookie sales."

Once the girl is gone, Vanessa closes the door. "God dammit," she says, "move." She tries to pull the bird off her shoulder, but its body feels so light and delicate she's afraid she'll crush it if she pulls too hard, so she lets it stay. A moment later her mother walks down the stairs, her hands filled with coins, her eyes focused on her cupped palms, concentrating on not letting any of the coins drop.

"I couldn't find my wallet, but this has to be enough for one box and then if you put me down for a dozen boxes I'll make sure to have a check waiting for you."

"What do you need twelve boxes of cookies for?" Vanessa asks, and Constance looks up. She doesn't like the sharpness of her daughter's tone.

"What have you done with Zephyr?"

"I murdered her and buried her under the porch."

"Don't be fresh with me."

"I gave her twenty dollars. She'll bring you four boxes when they come in."

"I wanted twelve boxes."

"Were you going to eat all those cookies?"

"Of course not, but what if I have guests?"

"When was the last time you had guests?" Nessie's eyes sweep around the living room, and Constance can tell she's judging, judging, judging.

"I'm just saying that if I did have guests, I'd like to be able to offer them something."

"Four boxes of cookies should suffice." It's time to ask; if she doesn't do it now, her sisters will arrive and then she'll have to ask them too since they're so attached to the house. She'll convince her mother that *Quick Fix Animal Collector* will be a dream come true. She'll get her mother to say yes before Jules and Jilly show up, and she'll make her mother sign the paperwork—which is in her bag—and then Jules and Jilly cannot tell their mother she can't do it. But just as she's about to ask, her sisters come crashing into the house, their voices loud, the swishing of the plastic Boston Market bags loud, their footsteps loud.

"Nessie!" they shout in unison. Vanessa is glad to note that at least today they are not dressed the same. The last time she came home for a holiday, Christmas in 2001, feeling vulnerable and in need of connection after watching the Twin Towers crumble from her apartment window a few months earlier, Jules and Jilly had been wearing matching sweaters featuring Mrs. Claus baking cookies. The sweaters seemed especially garish in light of the nation's suffering. Today Jules is wearing a blue and yellow polka-dotted polyester shirt and baggy acid washed jeans. Jilly is, strangely, wearing a Yankees sweatshirt, even though Vanessa knows she has never cared for sports. It must be a hand-me-down from her seventeen-year-old son, Noah, who, according to the pictures Jilly posts on Facebook on an annoyingly regular basis, is about a foot taller than his mother.

It is good to see Nessie, it really is, thinks Jules, as she drops the Boston Market bags in the kitchen and envelops Nessie in her arms. She feels a leather jacket and bones. "You're so skinny," she says. "Mom, look how skinny she is. Do they not have food in Manhattan?" Nessie looks so different from who she'd been as a child, so angular and sharp now.

"I eat enough," says Vanessa. She wishes she could fast forward through these uncomfortable greetings and skip to asking about filming the show. She is bracing herself for asking all three of them, for arguing with all three of them, for convincing all three of them.

Jilly asks, "How long are you home for?" She wants Nessie to stay, to be with them for a while. Nessie is always running off, running away. Jilly has always liked Nessie more than Jules has, but that's because Jilly and Jules are different. Jules chose to stay in their hometown. Jilly's situation is different. She hadn't meant to get pregnant at twenty by a boy she'd known in high school, had meant to meet someone exciting, maybe foreign, right after college, to sweep her off her feet and take her away from the place where she'd been born and lived in her entire life. She dreamed of a career as a singer, not a job as a middle school music teacher at the same middle school she attended. Jules and her husband, Leo, have no children, and they could leave, but Jules chooses to stay. And so Nessie's life is fascinating to Jilly—she's the one that got out—and Jilly wishes she wouldn't be so secretive, wishes she'd talk more about her life. She wishes Nessie would post updates on Facebook about her real life and not just about the shows she produces. She wishes Nessie would invite her down to visit, to stay in her apartment in the city for a few days. She wants to meet Nessie's friends, Nessie's boyfriends, but she—all of them—have been shut out of Nessie's life.

"I'm just here for a quick visit. I actually wanted to ask you something, Mom."

Here it comes, thinks Constance. But what could Nessie possibly want? She knows there's no money here, and she certainly doesn't want the house. And Constance is not so old that she needs to be put into some assisted living situation. What if Nessie *needs* something? Constance feels a flash of panic; after all, Nessie is her first born, and it is hard not to think of her as her baby, her very first baby. Nowadays she doesn't particularly like Nessie, but she loves her. What if she's so skinny because she's sick? What if she needs a kidney, or bone marrow? No, Constance thinks, it can't be that. She wouldn't want a part of any of them floating around inside her body.

"There's this new show I'm producing," Nessie begins, and Constance lets out a huge sigh of relief. Nessie is not ill. Thank the lord.

Vanessa tells her mother and sisters about the show, about how they'd fix the house, deal with the birds, redecorate. Her mother's face, which for a fleeting moment had looked strangely beatific, crimps. Jules shakes her head. Only Jilly looks excited, nodding.

"Will Grant Carpenter be involved?" Jilly asks. Grant Carpenter is a serious hunk, and it's funny that his last name is Carpenter and he's actually a carpenter. It's not a stage name; Jilly knows this from reading an interview with him in *People Magazine*. She is a little obsessed with him; she's even the moderator of the Fans of Grant Carpenter Facebook page.

"He'll probably be involved since he's the carpenter that works on most of the shows I produce." He's also Vanessa's favorite work friend. He's teaching her how to make things with wood. So far she has made a step stool and a spice rack, even though she almost never cooks and owns no spices beyond salt and pepper, and salt doesn't even count as a spice. But building things calms her nerves better than the prescription her doctor gave her that makes her feel dull and foggy. When Grant goes out of town, Vanessa watches his dog, a German shepherd named Hal. She knows Grant thinks she's doing him a favor, but she loves Hal's company, loves letting Hal sleep next to her, even though he snores loudly. Since she broke up with Yoshi two years ago and he took their French bulldog, Lulu, she's missed the presence of an animal in her apartment.

"I can't believe you know Grant Carpenter," Jilly says. She knows her voice has spiraled into a squeal, but the idea of having someone so famous, so handsome, and so talented right here in their mother's home is thrilling.

"You're married," Jules says. Jilly is such a nitwit, such a teenager. Jilly's students love her, and Jules thinks this is because she relates to them on their level. It's not like she needs to come down to their level, though; she's already there. She likes the same TV shows they like, listens to the same music they do. Jilly has lectured Jules on singers named Drake, Taylor Swift, and Cardi B, but Jules has no interest in hearing any of the songs Jilly plays when they drive together to their mother's house.

"I don't think Dwayne minds my having a little crush," Jilly says. "It's innocent."

Innocence, or more likely cluelessness, thinks Vanessa, is why Jilly has no idea Grant is gay. He lives with his partner of seven years, Ian, in a loft in Chelsea. This information isn't a secret but it's also not public knowledge. The CEO of the network insisted Grant keep his personal life quiet because there are plenty of female viewers who like to fantasize about strong, heterosexual carpenters. And now he's kept this secret for so long that he says it would feel strange making some big magazine-cover revelation. Vanessa has always felt sad about Grant having to keep that part of himself hidden from his fans, but now she looks at her sister and wonders what she'd think if she knew Grant is gay. She wonders if her family knows any gay people. She thinks about Yoshi, about how her family never met him, and wonders if her family knows anyone who is Japanese. She wonders what they would have thought if they'd known she was dating a Japanese man. She had always worried they'd have been small-minded, that they would have said offensive things.

"The show is a terrible idea," Constance says. She knows what will happen. They'll come in and touch her stuff. They'll move everything, they'll throw important things away. They'll take her birds. She has sixty-seven birds. They all have names. Some of them are related to each other.

"I agree with Mom," says Jules. What is Nessie thinking? How dare she march into their house and demand something like this?

"I think it could be fun," says Jilly. She smiles at Vanessa, and Vanessa realizes Jilly can be an ally in this fight. Jilly's lust for Grant Carpenter will be an asset. But, still, it's two against two; it's going to be a stalemate. So how can she convince Jules that this is a good idea? Responsible, bossy, penny-pinching Jules, who works as a financial manager at the bank and knows every way to stretch a dollar and has been investing her money since she was fourteen. Vanessa is sure Jules is going to be one of those people who dies with a secret multi-million dollar fortune, and everyone will say, "But she lived so frugally!" And then Vanessa has an idea.

"The renovations they do on *Quick Fix* usually range between one hundred and two hundred thousand dollars," Vanessa says. "And you wouldn't have to pay a cent of it." Vanessa is bending the truth; they usually try to keep the renovation costs far below a hundred thousand, but she's sure she can get plenty of sponsors to donate products that would add up to a hundred thousand—tubs, sinks, furniture, artwork—for free advertising. She'll figure it out.

"What would you fix in the house?" Jules asks. She has been trying to get her mother to repair the house for years. There are safety hazards everywhere. Sometimes Jules bolts awake from a nightmare of her mother's house burning, wiring gnawed by mice, sparks igniting the carpets, all the *Pennysavers* aflame, the house ablaze within minutes. The birds flying with flames sprouting from their wings. In the dreams she always hears the crackle and popping of all the burning birdseed. "Jules, Jules," says her husband, Leo, shaking her in bed. "The dream again?" he asks, and she nods, and he goes and warms some milk with honey for her and she feels better drinking the hot sweet milk and telling herself it's not real. But the dream *could* be real; there is so much in the house that could ignite. Since the dreams started, she's been wanting to clean the house, fix it, but how can she convince her bull-headed mother to allow her to do this? She knows it would be an expensive undertaking, and she's been saving money for five years in a secret account for house repairs. She's just never been sure how exactly to ask her mother to allow her to bring workers into the home.

"What do *you* think needs fixing?" Vanessa asks. She knows the best way to appeal to Jules is to ask her opinion, to act as if she's the only one with answers. Jules rattles off a long list: the stairs, the heating and cooling, pull up and replace the old carpeting with hardwood, check all the wiring, get the fireplace in working condition again . . .

"Hold on," says Vanessa, rustling around in her bag for a notebook, "let me take notes." She doesn't really care what Jules's list is, but she knows taking notes on what Jules is saying will help convince her.

"This sounds like a wonderful idea," Jilly says. She can't believe they'll be on television. Her students won't believe it when she tells them on Monday. She knows quite a few watch *Quick Fix*. She's a little worried about *Animal Collectors*, knows they might not portray her mother in the best way. They usually show the people on *Animal Collectors* as not understanding why their animals are a problem, and Jilly knows her mother can be a crank, will argue with the therapist they bring in to talk to her about her hoarding. But maybe it will all turn out to be a good thing; maybe this will be what they need to finally get this place cleaned up and the bird situation sorted out.

Jules thinks of the money she will not have to personally spend on this. It's always been her money that's spent whenever their mother needs something; she's always been the responsible one. There is ninety thousand dollars in the account for house repairs. It's money Jules already considered spent, so now this is like a ninety-thousand-dollar windfall. Maybe she will buy her dream car, a red Jaguar F-TYPE Coupe, and the girls at the bank will not believe it when they see her rolling up in it. Or maybe she'll take a vacation. She and Leo will go to Europe. No, scratch that. Leo would hate Europe. She'll take Leo to Cooperstown, be patient while he moves slowly through the Baseball Hall of Fame. And then she'll take him on a tour of that Ommegang brewery because he loves their beer, and then he'll be happy to come home and plop down into his La-Z-Boy. Then she'll go to Europe with Libby and Ellen, her friends from the bank. She'll pay for them, and they'll be stunned. They'll start in Paris, will eat rich buttery pastries and drink dark luscious wine. They will climb to the top of the Eiffel Tower. They will watch mimes perform in the street, and Jules will confess that she has always wanted to learn to mime, and her friends will find this revelation to be both surprising and delightful. They will go to the Louvre and look at the *Mona Lisa*. She knows these are clichéd things people do when they go to Paris, but she thinks if it's your first time there, it's what you need to do. "It might not be a terrible idea to have some work done on the house," says Jules.

Constance looks at her daughters. How odd that all three of them are agreeing to this. How strange that they're all on the same page. They are never on the same page. She feels, suddenly, ganged-up on. "No one is taking my birds," she says. "I love my birds." Right now she loves her birds more than she loves her girls.

The goddamn birds, Vanessa thinks. If they are the chess piece that can't be moved, then fine, they'll work around the birds. Maybe Grant can make an elaborate set of birdcages that can be put outside. They'll deal with the birds later. And maybe Gretchen, the psychologist who works with many of the animal collectors, can convince her mother that no one needs this many birds.

"If they don't move your birds, will you sign the paperwork?" Vanessa says. "And maybe we can have the carpenter make some nice cages for the birds."

Jilly nods. It's a good idea for her mother to do this. And she's certain Grant can construct beautiful cages for the birds. She'll offer herself up to help. Maybe she can bring Noah. Her son could learn a thing or two. His only passion is playing video games. She would love it if her boy could make cabinets and chairs and tables.

Maybe he'll discover a love of carpentry. Maybe Grant Carpenter will take him on as an apprentice. Noah's grades certainly aren't going to get him into college, and she fears if she doesn't figure out a path for him, she'll find him slumped on the couch in her living room for the rest of his life, the video game controller always warm from his touch.

Constance looks at her girls, all three of them together in the kitchen for the first time in who knows how long. They are all standing in a row, nodding at her like a bunch of bobble-heads. She hates the idea and knows deep in her gut that something will happen to her birds. But when was the last time all three girls wanted the same thing? And this will keep Nessie around for a bit, and Constance knows how Jilly has always wanted to spend more time with her big sister. She knows she will regret it, but after a few moments of staring at their hopeful faces, she says, "Okay, fine. If you must."

Jilly cannot believe it has all come to be, only two weeks after her mother agreed to this. There are cameramen and men with large microphones they hold over their heads, and two men are setting up an extension cord with hanging lights so the living room is better illuminated. Nessie is ordering people around and Jilly is impressed because it's nice ordering, keeping things in control without being bossy. Nessie is wearing a checked red flannel shirt, but it looks classy; it fits well without gaping and it's tucked in, and she looks professional and in charge. She is wearing glasses with thick brown frames. Jilly didn't know Nessie wore glasses. "Go ask your aunt if she needs any help," Jilly says to Noah.

"Mom, it's not like she's setting the table for dinner," Noah says. "She's *working*."

Nessie turns to them, waves Noah over to her. "Can I borrow him?" she asks.

Jilly nods.

"We're going to interview you about Grandma, okay?" Vanessa says.

"What should I say?" says Noah.

"Just answer the questions," says Vanessa. "We're going to ask about the birds and about whether you like coming over here."

"I don't want Grandma getting mad at me if I tell the truth."

Vanessa bites her lip. Noah is a good kid, she knows that, but he's like his father: tentative, hesitant. Maybe like his mother too: unadventurous, complacent.

"How about this?" Vanessa says. "We'll film it and then later we'll let you watch the footage we plan to use, and if you don't like it, we won't use it?"

Noah nods, and Vanessa feels a flicker of guilt. If he says anything juicy, if he reveals how much he hates being in this filthy house, *of course* they'll use it. The more conflict there is, the better the ratings will be. She'll tell him they'll cut it and then when it appears on TV, she'll say she had no idea they were going to use that footage. It doesn't matter if he's mad at her; they hardly see each other, are nearly strangers to one another.

Vanessa walks Noah to a corner of the living room where a large bright light has been set up by the gaffer, and Mary, another producer, clips a mic onto Noah's shirt and asks her first question. The interview is filmed. Vanessa knows that although Mary has a round face and deep dimples and looks like Shirley Temple, she's really a shark. She always gets people to cry when she interviews them. At first, when Mary had been hired, Vanessa thought Mary was too manipulative, too intent on getting a good story, but now she sees this is what viewers want. They want tears, they want big confessions, they want drama.

Dustin, the sound mixer, comes up to Vanessa shaking his head. "These birds," he says, "it's all you can hear. All that squawking and wing flapping. I can barely hear what people are saying."

"Can it be taken out in post-production?" Vanessa asks. The birds seem louder than ever; maybe they're nervous with all these people in the house.

"I'll try, but I can't guarantee anything," says Dustin. He points to three birds that are skidding across the living room table. "How does she live with this?"

"I don't know," Vanessa says. She remembers when she first moved to New York City for college her mother asked her how she could sleep at night with all the activity right outside her window, the cabs and ambulances whooshing down the street at all hours, the people wandering around shouting drunkenly, the music floating over from the bar across the street. Back then, her mother hadn't started with the birds. Back then, her mother was still normal. Vanessa told her mother she hardly noticed the city noise, but that wasn't true. For her entire first year in the city she had trouble sleeping, missed the crickets she could hear from her bedroom in this house. But after that first year she'd adjusted, and now the night sounds of the city are soothing, make her feel as if she's not alone, that she's part of a busy and full world.

"How about you film most of the interviews outdoors?" Vanessa says. "It'll be quieter."

"Your mom doesn't keep any birds outside?" Dustin asks.

"She says if they go outside they might decide to fly away."

Jilly stands in the center of the living room watching Vanessa talk to the sound guy. She feels both useless and on edge, doesn't know what to do with herself. Jules took their mother to IHOP for breakfast. Nessie asked that one of them take their mother out while the house was prepared for filming. Jilly has not yet seen her mother today, but she's certain she must be nervous and upset. Jilly moves to the couch so she can look out the window and see when her mother returns with Jules.

Vanessa gets a text from Grant, who is five minutes away. He drove upstate in a rental car. Vanessa looks at Jilly, who is kneeling on the couch and looking out the front window. She is wearing makeup, bright red lipstick, rouge, blue eye shadow. She is obviously anticipating Grant's arrival, peering out the window like an excited puppy waiting for its owner to come home. She reminds

Vanessa of Lulu and the way she sat upright and at attention by the apartment door every night, eagerly awaiting Yoshi's return from work.

Jilly cannot believe it: Grant Carpenter is emerging from a car in front of her mother's house. He's taller than he looks on TV, which is strange because she's heard celebrities are usually much shorter than they appear to be on television. And movie stars are even worse. She's heard Tom Cruise is puny and he always wears lifts in his shoes. Jilly pops up from the couch and straightens her skirt.

Vanessa watches Grant stride up the walkway. Her heart is pounding. She should have requested another carpenter for this shoot. She doesn't want Grant to know she has come from this. Even though she has opened up to him about a lot of things she hasn't told anyone else about—the breakup with Yoshi; the brief, terrible period in her early twenties when she was a newscaster in Syracuse; how during college she was a contestant in one ill-advised beauty pageant, with the hope of earning tuition money—she doesn't want to let him into this part of her life.

"Hello, hello, welcome," says Jilly, and she sticks out a hand for Grant to shake. "I am such a *huge* fan." No, she tells herself. Rein it in. Calm down.

"You must be Jillian," Grant says, and for the first time ever Jilly thinks the name Jillian sounds beautiful and sophisticated. Instead of shaking her hand, Grant envelops her in a hug, and his arms feel strong and he smells good, like cedar. "So great to meet you," he says, and Jilly's heart thumps because he is real and he is standing in front of her and he is even more handsome than he looks on TV.

Vanessa is thankful Jilly is not panting with excitement, like Lulu always did when Yoshi reached for her leash. "We were thinking it might work to build a bunch of cages outdoors so my mother could keep a good number of her birds outside. Jilly, would you take Grant outside and show him the backyard?"

Jilly smiles and nods. Vanessa thinks the backyard is less embarrassing than the indoors. It is not well kept, but at least it's not
covered in bird shit and it doesn't smell. She looks over at Noah
in the corner being interviewed and, predictably, he's crying.

Next door, Zephyr watches the action from her bedroom
window. There's Jilly and she's in the backyard with the carpenter she has seen on TV at her friend Gabriella's house. Zephyr's
family does not own a TV. Zephyr knows this means she has
read more books than most of her classmates and that she can
entertain herself by drawing or making something out of clay
or trying to train one of the chickens to walk backward, but still,
she'd rather have a TV so she can know what everyone is talking
about at school when they discuss the shows they watch. Lately,
Zephyr has been annoyed with her family, and her mother calls
her "angsty." But right now her family is highly unsatisfactory.
Her mother is a photographer and is working on a project doc-
umenting abandoned buildings in the Hudson Valley. She's gone
so often; her project involves photographing the same buildings
in the sunlight and in the dark of night, so sometimes she takes
her sleeping bag and camps out overnight in the abandoned
buildings. This year, Zephyr thinks her mother has spent more
nights in these abandoned buildings than she has at home. Zephyr
worries about bears and foxes and coyotes finding her mother.
She worries about bad people finding and harming her mother.
Since her mother is gone all the time, Zephyr's left with her father
and three brothers, and she has had just about enough of Dash,
Satchel, and Sage. She wishes she had sisters. Or even one sister.
She's jealous of Jilly and Jules and Vanessa. And with Constance
that makes four females. When she complains to her brothers
that she's surrounded by too many boys, they tell her to go play
with the chickens. "They're all girls, except for Roy," Sage tells her.
Roy is their loud rooster. But of course chickens and sisters are
not the same thing. Chickens are not actually very fun to have
as pets; they cannot be trained like dogs can, although they do

give you eggs. Eggs! She will bring over some eggs. This will be her excuse for joining the fun next door.

As Constance and Jules pull up the block toward her house, Constance sees three vans in her driveway. On the other side of the house are two large dumpsters. There are people bustling in and out of the house. A man is holding open the front door while another man carries in a box of electrical cords. "The birds!" she says, and Jules says, "Nessie said they won't get rid of the birds. I'll hold her to it."

"If they leave the front door open, the birds will fly out," says Constance.

"I'll take care of it," says Jules. She pulls up behind one of the large white vans in the driveway and turns off the engine. She charges out of the car, and Constance knows her daughter is glad to have a mission, to be able to tell others what to do. Jules is the youngest of all her daughters. She is twelve minutes younger than Jilly, yet Jules has always acted as if she's the oldest of them all.

Inside, Constance sees some of the birds—the dumber ones, like little gray Huey—nosing around, bopping over the equipment, trying to make friends. Huey seems enamored with a large fluffy microphone. The smart birds have hidden themselves away.

"Your sister had a great idea," Grant says, as he enters the house through the back door.

"Jilly?" says Vanessa. "Where is she?"

"Out back," says Grant. He points to the backyard with a thumb. "She's got my measuring tape. She's taking measurements. Her kid is out there too, helping out."

"Is he still crying?" Vanessa says.

"A little. Mary should lay off, especially with kids."

"It makes for good TV, though," Vanessa says, shrugging.

"Good TV isn't always the most important thing."

Vanessa doesn't like his patronizing tone. "You know my sister is in love with you, right?"

"I got the sense that she's a fan."

"I think she likes you because you're so different from her husband. He reminds me of a dumpling."

"Like a potsticker?" Grant looks confused.

"There's just something dumplingish about him. Pale. Soft. Smooshy."

Vanessa wonders why she is being unkind. Maybe subconsciously she believes the meaner she is about her family, the more she can distance herself from them. It is time to change the subject. "What was Jilly's idea?"

"We're going to build cages outside that look like an apartment building. I was thinking New York City, but Jilly said Paris. I was picturing fire escapes, but Jilly suggested balconies. She said she's always wanted to go to Paris."

"Tiny little bird balconies. Do you have time for that?"

"We'll figure it out. Her son can help. He says he might want to be a carpenter."

All of it is news to her: Jilly's interest in Paris, Noah's interest in carpentry.

"Jilly and I can take one of the vans and go to the hardware store for supplies," Grant says. "Noah will stay here and look up and print out photographs of Parisian apartment buildings we can use as a reference. Jilly said your mom has a computer and printer."

"Okay," says Vanessa. She is unsure if this plan to build delicate little Parisian birdhouses will work, but she's already run her mouth too much. And, after all, maybe it won't happen; maybe Noah will spend all day looking for the computer and printer in the mess of the house and will give up his search in disgust before he can print out photos for Grant to use as references.

Jules leads Noah up to her mother's bedroom. It is a disaster, the stained mattress with no sheets, the garbage can overflowing, empty plastic grocery bags everywhere. There are several bags of birdseed that have been pecked open, the seeds spilling onto the already soiled carpet. Jules thinks she sees the thin tail of a mouse disappear beneath a pile of shoes. The room is musty, airless. How does her mother sleep in here? How can she wake up to this mess every morning? Despite all the people in the house, despite the chaos today, she is grateful this is happening. The house will be cleaned, and this will be good for her mother. Jules knows the hoarding was triggered by her father leaving. Her mother hadn't expected it, and even all these years later she still isn't over it. Her father was the love of her mother's life. But he tossed away their marriage for a woman he met in a hotel bar on a business trip to Vegas. The birds, Jules understands, fill some sort of void for her mother, keep her occupied and distracted. She bought her first bird the day after their father left.

"Whoa," says Noah. "That computer is ancient." They look at an old blue-and-white iMac from the nineties. "Are you sure it's connected to the Internet?"

"Your grandma said there's AOL on there. She still has a dial-up connection, though."

Noah shakes his head. He takes his cell phone out of his pocket and takes a picture of the computer. "My friends are not going to believe this."

"Don't post that picture anywhere," Jules says. She grabs the phone out of Noah's hand and tries to figure out how to delete the photo. The boy looks hurt, his large green eyes wide.

"I'm sorry," says Jules, giving the phone back to her nephew. "I didn't mean to snap at you. It's just this room, well, we don't want people to see it, do we?"

"But they'll see it anyway on TV, won't they? Aunt Jules, I should have said no when that lady wanted to interview me. Now I'm going to be on TV and everyone at school is going to laugh at me."

"Why would they laugh at you?"

"Because I cried. And because they'll see inside this house and they'll have proof that she really is the crazy bird lady. Why do you think kids throw rotten eggs at her house every Halloween?"

"They throw rotten eggs?"

Noah nods, then covers his mouth with his hand. "Oh, I didn't mean to tell you. It just slipped out."

"Tell me what happens with the eggs," says Jules.

"My mom said I'm not supposed to tell you."

"Tell me. Please."

Noah sighs. "Every year after midnight on Halloween my mom and I come by and get the hose out and clean off the eggs as much as we can."

"Does Grandma know?" Jules asks.

"I guess she can hear the kids screaming outside, calling her the crazy bird lady. And she can probably hear the water from the hose. But Mom and me, we've never talked to her about it."

"Why haven't you ever told me about this?" Why has Jilly kept this a secret all these years? She could have come over and helped. Leo would have helped too, would have brought a bucket and sponges and helped wipe down the siding and windows.

Noah says, "My mom says she knows you like giving out candy on Halloween. And this would ruin your Halloween."

Jules thinks about all those years when she's sat in her living room wearing a pair of black cat ears, waiting for trick-or-treaters to come by so she can put king-sized candy bars into their bags and plastic pumpkins. Halloween makes her feel good, makes her feel extravagant; those king-sized bars have always seemed like an appropriate way to spend her money. She has harbored thoughts that the children in her neighborhood say her house is the best house for trick-or-treating and talk about her generosity. But all these years while she was waiting to give away candy, Jilly was gearing up to clean eggs off their mother's house. She feels a swell of love for her twin. "She wanted to protect me," Jules says.

"Yeah," Noah says, "that's what she says every year. 'We'll protect your aunt from this unpleasantness.'"

Jilly is in a van with Grant Carpenter. It is just the two of them, zipping down the street and Jilly wants so badly to roll down the windows and shout, "Look who I'm with! Look who's in our town! Look who's going to fix my mother's house!" But of course she says nothing.

Grant fiddles with the knob of the air conditioning. "The AC is shot," he says.

"Left here," says Jilly. She is directing Grant to Lowe's, where they will pick up all the supplies they need for the birdhouses. The Parisian birdhouses. She can hear Grant breathing, a slight whistle coming out of his nose, and this puts her at ease. He is on TV but he is human. And he's her sister's friend. She wonders what he knows about her sister that she does not know. "Another left," Jilly says.

"Vanessa told me you run my fan page on Facebook."

Jilly's face grows warm. She's sure she seems silly to him, someone with not enough to do, practically a stalker. "It's just something I do for fun," she says. "I hope you don't mind."

"Of course not," he says. "I'm grateful."

"Oh, you don't have to say that," Jilly says. "I know it's silly."

"It's not. I hate social media, all the pettiness of it, all the boasting. I quit Facebook years ago, so you're doing me a favor."

"Can I ask you something?" Jilly says. She wants to ask about Nessie's life in the city, about how she spends her time. She wants to see what Grant will tell her.

"It's true," he says. "And it's okay if anyone wants to say anything about it on the Facebook page. I'm tired of hiding."

"What's true?" says Jilly, but she suspects she knows what he's getting at. But she wants him to say it just to make sure. She has spent time deleting comments on the Facebook page from people who want to dig into Grant's personal life. It's his business who he wants to date, and it's his business what he wants people to know about his life.

"I have a partner. His name is Ian," says Grant.

People are always telling Jilly their secrets. Students confide in her about crushes, parents who put too much pressure on them, cheating on tests, friends who turn out to be bad influences. Jilly tries to listen closely to her students, to offer what advice she can, to not judge. The guidance counselors at the middle school joke with Jilly, tell her the students spill more to her than they do in the guidance office. "You're the music teacher," they always say. "They should be asking you about what instruments they should play!" But music is about passion and heart, the big things in life, and maybe that's why the students feel comfortable opening up to her.

"Ian, that was the guy you were photographed with at the farmers' market?" she says. She saw the photo in *Us Weekly* and thought of scanning it and posting it on the Facebook page, but she knew questions would arise about the relationship between the two of them.

"That's him."

"He's very handsome," says Jilly. Not as handsome as Grant, of course, but, still, a strong-jawed, tall, good-looking man. "And the dog?"

"That's Hal. Our dog."

They pull into the parking lot of Lowe's and get out of the car. Jilly can feel people staring at them. She sees people raising their cell phones to take pictures.

"Does Nessie know? Vanessa, I mean."

Grant nods. He pulls a shopping cart from a line of carts. "Vanessa's one of our best friends. She dog sits for us. It's been hard on her since Yoshi took Lulu away. Sometimes we lie and tell her we're going out of town so she'll take Hal for the weekend. She always seems happier after a few days with Hal."

Who are Yoshi and Lulu? Jilly is silent. There is so much running through her mind: Grant has confirmed he is gay, there is a Yoshi, there is a Lulu.

"You still don't know? About Yoshi?" Grant says.

Jilly shakes her head. Grant pushes the cart past the lighting aisle. "Vanessa and Yoshi were together for six years," he says.

"Nessie's not so forthcoming about her life. At least not with us," Jilly says. "Is Lulu their daughter?" She might have a niece, a secret little niece in New York City. The thought delights her, even though knowing Vanessa has kept so much of her life a secret infuriates her.

Grant laughs. "No, no. Yoshi was her boyfriend. Lulu was their dog. I thought she would have at least told you she was with someone, even if she didn't introduce him to you. Yoshi got the dog in the breakup."

"How long ago was that?"

"Two years. Yoshi and I used to run in the park together after he got off work. He's a pharmacist. We were good friends. After the breakup he moved to San Francisco, and I haven't seen him since then."

"Why'd they break up?"

They turn down the lumber aisle. Grant loads dowels and thin boards of wood into the cart. "He was upset that Vanessa never introduced him to her family, to you, your sister, your mom. He thought she was hiding him. He thought she was embarrassed that he was Japanese. He thought maybe your family was racist."

"Oh," says Jilly. "We're not. We're not racist at all." She thinks about each year's cultural immersion week at the middle school, how two years ago the school studied Japan, how she learned about Bunraku puppetry and worked with the art teacher to put together a puppet show. The students ate sushi brought in from Price Chopper, which Jilly knew was not good sushi, but they were able to get a bulk discount. They planted a cherry blossom tree in the garden behind the school. And maybe this all happened during the time Nessie was breaking up with Yoshi. "Also," Jilly adds, "we're not, um, homophobic."

Grant nods. "I know," he says.

"If she'd just introduced us to Yoshi, maybe things would be different," Jilly says. She thinks of Nessie with Yoshi, with a dog.

She tries to picture Nessie happy, smiling, throwing a Frisbee to a dog in a park. But she can't.

"Families are difficult," Grant says. They are now in the aisle with the paints and stains, and Grant loads a dozen cans of wood stain and several paintbrushes into the cart.

"Is your family difficult?"

"They're in Missouri. I don't talk to them much."

They head to the registers and Jilly feels heavy, defeated. She wants to hug Grant because she sees how sad he is about his difficult family and about losing his friendship with Yoshi, but she cannot just stop and hug him in the middle of Lowe's. Her feet hurt; her toes are pinched in her dress shoes. She thinks of the whole life Nessie has had without letting them into it. She thinks of Nessie's heart being broken, about Yoshi and Lulu in San Francisco. And she thinks of how little she knows her sister, how all those years of wishing to know her better, to be closer to her, have resulted in this: her sister has hidden so much from her. Her sister is a stranger.

Nessie is wearing a pair of yellow dishwashing gloves and is putting Constance's Cool Whip containers into large black garbage bags. Constance feels a tug in her chest; she feels that what's important is being taken away. All morning men have been hauling garbage bags out to the dumpster. "No, no," Constance says, but the men don't listen to her. "We have a job to do, ma'am," says a man with a thick brown beard.

"Let's go outside, Constance," says Dr. Gretchen, the show's psychiatrist. "Let's go get some air." What is this, kindergarten? Dr. Gretchen surely has a last name, Constance thinks. Dr. Gretchen leads Constance outside to the backyard, unfolds two plastic chairs, and Constance sits in one chair and Dr. Gretchen the other. "How do you feel, Constance?" A cameraman is recording everything.

"How the hell do you think I feel?" Constance snaps. She will not say her feelings out loud for this woman and for the world to see. They can clean her kitchen but she will not be made to spill the contents of her mind.

"How does seeing your possessions go into the dumpster make you feel?" Dr. Gretchen asks.

Constance glowers at Dr. Gretchen. She can keep asking questions. Constance will not answer. Her arms are itchy, and she scratches them, pulls up the sleeves of her sweatshirt. She has hives. They're from stress. The year Stanley left her, she had hives nearly every day. She suspects Dr. Gretchen will think they're from being dirty, from mouse feces and bird diseases getting on her skin, but that's not the case. They are stress hives.

"Grandma?" says Noah, and Constance looks up at him. He's holding a few pages of paper with images he's printed from her computer. The ink is faded. She needs to refill the ink in the printer. She remembers buying a big package with four ink cartridges but she can't remember where she put it. "I'm printing out images of how the birdhouses will look. These are some apartment buildings in Paris. What do you think?"

Constance takes the pages from Noah. These buildings look complicated. Will they really be able to make birdcages that look like Parisian apartment buildings? Her birds don't want to be in cages. They like to fly free around the house. And how will she feed the birds? Will she have to feed each bird in each cage individually? She likes to leave a large bowl of birdseed in the middle of the dining room table and the birds can eat whenever they're hungry.

"Aunt Jules left to go pick up Uncle Leo," Noah says. "He's going to help us make the birdhouses. We'll have to make a lot, so the more helpers the better."

Constance's hives itch again. She scratches her arms. And now her head is itchy, but she knows if she scratches her head it'll be over. There will be talk of lice or fleas. She balls her hands into fists. She will not scratch her head. She will not.

"Hi, Constance!" It is the little girl from next door. She is holding a basket of eggs, tilting them toward Constance. There must be twenty eggs in there, brown and white and some green ones with darker green speckles. No, no, this is not how things work. She is never given eggs in the light of day. One of the Duncan boys, the tallest one, the one with the funny haircut that makes him look like a Gloster canary, comes early in the morning, before the rest of the block is awake, and deposits a basket of eggs on Constance's doorstep. These eggs are a silent thank you because Constance will not complain about the Duncans' rooster crowing. She likes the secretness of the exchange, likes how no one has ever said anything even though everyone understood what was going on. And now this girl, this dumb girl, is holding a basket of eggs out to Constance, and it feels like everything that had been secret and quiet has been spilled out, made public. And once the show airs, everything will be even worse. Constance knows what the neighborhood children say about her. And now they'll have proof, on tape, of her uncleanliness, of her craziness.

"I brought you eggs!" the girl says, a smile stretched across her face.

Constance wants to say *Take them away* but instead her hands go to her head and she begins to scratch, hard, and she hears the psychiatrist, the goddamned Dr. Gretchen, say, "This behavior is to be expected," and Constance thinks of how no one here understands anything about her, about how difficult her life has been, about how the birds are the biggest comfort to her, and then she begins to weep.

Vanessa sees her mother crying and understands what a profound mistake she's made. Now she's so deep into the shoot she can't cancel, can't backtrack without looking irresponsible and flighty, wasteful of the network's money. She needs to see this through if she doesn't want to lose her job. She sees her mother scratching, first her head, then her arms. Vanessa kneels by her mother, puts her hand on her mother's thigh. "Do you have any Benadryl in the house?"

She nods, then shakes her head. "I don't know where it is," she whispers.

Vanessa looks up and sees a cameraman still filming. "Could you stop for a minute?" she says. "My mom is having an allergic reaction."

"It's likely stress-induced," says Gretchen. "Does she have any prescriptions for anti-anxiety meds?"

"Could you go get her some Benadryl?" Vanessa asks. "She needs an antihistamine." No one moves. Everyone just stares at her and her mother. Vanessa is on her knees still, the moisture from the grass seeping into her jeans. Her mother keeps crying. "Someone!" she barks. "Someone go find my mother some Benadryl!"

"We might have some," says Zephyr. "In our house." It is a lie; her family does not use any medicine from the drugstore, but they have a salve made of olive oil and chickweed that can be rubbed on itchy spots.

"Could you go get it?" says Vanessa. The girl nods and puts the basket of eggs down at Constance's feet. Constance looks at the eggs and starts crying harder. "Could you take these eggs away?" Vanessa asks. She doesn't know why the eggs are upsetting her mother, but they are.

"I'll go," says Mary. For the first time ever, Vanessa is grateful to Mary. Maybe she's the producer that can make the most interviewees cry, but she's also the only one who is making any moves to help.

"There's a cvs right up the street," says Constance, but she is crying so hard that it's difficult for her to talk and she wonders if the producer has even understood what she said.

"I'll get you some tissues," Vanessa says, and Constance nods. Vanessa will not ask her mother where the tissues are; she'll find them inside somehow.

In the living room, Dustin waves Vanessa over to a computer set up on a table in the corner of the room. "Listen," he says and presses play. Vanessa sees Noah on the screen, blinking back tears. He says, "I just wish people would understand my grandma isn't a big weirdo. She just really loves the birds." Vanessa knows immediately this footage will be used. She knows that once it airs, the kids at school will make fun of Noah. She stares at her nephew's pale round face and thinks again of dumplingness, and this time she thinks of how being tender and dumpling-like isn't a bad thing. Noah is sensitive and kind, like his father. Like Jilly too.

"I was able to get rid of the bird sounds," Dustin says. "I seriously didn't think I would be able to do it, but I tried out this new program." He plays the snippet again, and there is only silence in the background.

"We could always put some of the chirps back in if the quietness is too unbelievable." Dustin replays the clip of Noah blinking back tears, insisting his grandmother is not a weirdo. It is so strange to watch the video of Noah in her mother's living room with the complete absence of bird sounds. And then Vanessa thinks maybe the birds have been for her mother what the city noises are to her: a soundtrack to her days and nights, noise to keep her distracted and fill the large, painful gaps in her life. When Vanessa was young, her father was the one who filled the house with noise. He told booming, unfunny jokes, but he was so invested in his jokes that all of them—the three girls and their mother—could not help but laugh along with him. He played guitar, not well, but they sang folk songs, like "Scarborough Fair" and "If I Had a Hammer" and "Puff the Magic Dragon." Her sisters are still loud, heavy-footed, but they no longer live here; they have their own busy lives outside this house. Dustin presses "play" again, and the silence in the recording, the complete lack of birdcalls, sounds devastating to Vanessa.

Zephyr picks up the basket of eggs and slowly walks into and through the house, watching everything the film crew is doing. There are many vans in the driveway, plus the dumpsters are on the other side of the house, so it is easiest to walk through the house to get from the backyard to the front. She exits through the front door and stands on Constance's lawn. She's afraid she'll miss something exciting if she goes home, but she'll take the eggs home and bring back the salve for Constance's itchy arms. She wants to be helpful. She knows that by leaving twenty eggs on the counter, she's going to inspire her father to make a giant frittata for dinner. Frittatas are one of the three dinners he knows how to make. She's tired of frittatas; she wishes her mother would come home.

While she's crossing the lawn on the way to her house, the woman comes back from the drugstore up the street with a plastic bag containing Benadryl. Jules returns with her husband, and they park their blue car in front of the house. Jilly comes back with the carpenter and they unload lumber from the back of a white van. There are so many people going into and out of the house all at once and the front door is being held open by one of the cameramen so Jilly and the carpenter can get all the wood into the front door and then out the back to build the birdcages in the backyard. And while the door is open, the birds begin to fly out. At first it is one bird at a time, and no one besides Zephyr seems to notice with all the commotion—the carrying in of the lumber, the introductions of Jules's husband, the shaking of the bottle of Benadryl tablets—and then when the adults turn their heads it is too late, the birds darting out in large groups.

"Oh no!" says Jules, pointing to the air.

The carpenter drops the lumber he's carrying and it clatters loudly. He tries to reach up to catch a bird, but of course that doesn't work. The birds flap and fly, up, up, up.

It is beautiful, Zephyr thinks, a flash of colors rising. There is a rainbow of birds now lined up on the electrical wires above the house. There are other birds flying away, flapping until Zephyr can no longer see them in the distance.

"Come back!" screams Jilly, waving her arms. "No!"

Zephyr wishes her mother were here to take photographs of the escaped birds. She wants to run home for a camera, but she thinks that by the time she gets back all the birds might be gone, so she just stands still, holding the basket of eggs. Then Vanessa and Constance appear at the front door. Following them are a cameraman and a soundman hoisting a large microphone.

"They're gone," wails Constance. "They're all gone."

"Some will come back," says Vanessa. "This is their home." She hopes this is true, but she doesn't really believe they will return. A cameraman is outside filming the birds on the wire, and she is certain this shot—including her mother's grief—will be shown on television, and she wants to wail, too, for the irreparable damage she has caused.

Constance shakes her head. She thought she'd given the birds a good life, a good home, but maybe all these years they were all longing to escape, to fly free. She knows how it goes: once they leave they won't return. Her chest feels tight, pained, and she lifts her hand to her heart. "They're all gone," she says again.

But this is not true. Zephyr can see that someone has not left. Behind Constance, the gray bird—the one who perched on Vanessa's shoulder and then on Zephyr's clipboard—sits on the fuzzy microphone. He stares at Constance, head tilted. He looks like he's waiting for her to speak, waiting for her to explain everything that has happened, because what's in front of him is puzzling and impossible to comprehend.

ACKNOWLEDGMENTS

I am grateful to the following journals and their editors who first published the stories in this collection:

"Still Life" in *Virginia Quarterly Review*
"Housekeeping" in *The Southern Review*
"Roland Raccoon" in *New Ohio Review*
"Perspective for Artists" in *Bellingham Review*
"Since Vincent Left" in *Crazyhorse*
"Aquatics" in *Hayden's Ferry Review*
"Lost or Damaged" in *Boulevard*
"Migration" in *Story*

Thank you to MacDowell, the Saltonstall Foundation for the Arts, the Sewanee Writers Conference, and the Longleaf Writers Conference for their support while I wrote these stories. I'm also appreciative of the support I received from the Committee on Teaching and Faculty Development and the English Department at Siena College as I worked on this collection. Finally, I'd like to express my gratitude to Kwame Dawes and Siwar Masannat at *Prairie Schooner* and Courtney Ochsner, Abby Goodwin, Ann Baker, and everyone else at the University of Nebraska Press for the time, attention, and care they gave to this book.

To order or obtain more information on these or other
University of Nebraska Press titles, visit nebraskapress.unl.edu.